Moses Unchained

Marilyn F. Moriarty

MOSES UNCHAINED

The University of Georgia Press   Athens & London

Published by the University of Georgia Press
Athens, Georgia 30602
© 1998 by Marilyn F. Moriarty
Designed by Sandra Strother Hudson
Set in New Caledonia by Graphic Composition, Inc.
Printed and bound by Maple-Vail
The paper in this book meets the guidelines for
permanence and durability of the Committee on
Production Guidelines for Book Longevity of the
Council on Library Resources.

Printed in the United States of America
98 99 00 01 02 C 5 4 3 2 1

Library of Congress Cataloging in Publication Data
Moriarty, Marilyn F.
Moses unchained / Marilyn F. Moriarty.
    p.   cm.
ISBN 0-8203-1985-6 (alk. paper)
I. Title.
  PS3563.O871636M67   1998
  813'.54—dc21   97-40787

British Library Cataloging in Publication Data available

Frontispiece: *Vision on the Mesa* © 1997 by Terry Rowlett

Winner of the Associated Writing Programs Award
for Creative Nonfiction

Moses Unchained

Introduction

It started with a cup of blood.

The consecrated blood of the Mass. December 6, 1993, the feast of St. Nicholas, Giver of Gifts. St. Nicholas was the patron saint of the Healing Light Center in Roanoke, Virginia, where I went to develop my spirituality. That year, the feast of St. Nicholas fell on a week night, so Father Dan planned a special celebration. Having arrived early, I waited in a meeting room for Mass to start. An English professor at a private liberal arts college, I had a pile of papers to read while I waited. A tall man, nearly six feet, walked into the room. He looked my age, early forties. His big brown eyes sparkled like star sapphires. A woolly, red beard down to his chest covered his black leather vest. Under the vest he wore a red-and-black-checked flannel shirt and jeans and over the vest a wool coat. A silly hat, like a beat-up fedora, was cocked on his head. When he crossed the room, his footsteps sounded heavy; he wore steel-toed boots. Workingman's boots. I wondered why anyone would wear boots to church. I didn't know at the time that they were his only shoes.

"I'm looking for the priest," he said.

I said that Father Dan was probably getting ready for Mass. If the stranger wanted, he could attend. He looked around, hands deep in his pockets, fidgeting as we talked. Finally, he blurted out: "I got an honorable testimony."

I listened to Zack and his honorable testimony — a testimony from the Baptist perspective with Old Testament overtones, his bearing witness to the active role God played in his life.

When it was time for Mass, I asked Zack if he wanted to go with me; he said yes, though he had never been to one before. The church wasn't crowded, only a few people scattered in pews.

I handed Zack a missal. He read the prayers. He followed the refrains. He whispered to me, "This is like a play." Then it was time for Communion.

Eight or ten people went to the front for Communion. We stood in a circle around Father Dan, who had stepped down from the altar. He held a chalice full of hosts and a chalice full of wine. The wine chalice shone yellow-gold, that rich metallic color you see on the domes of basilicas. Those receiving communion passed the wine chalice around. Zack was to my right, and he drank first. Then he passed the cup to me. I held it up to my mouth and looked in. At the bottom swirled red wine, made deeper by the gold color of the chalice. I remember at the time it looked like blood. I thought to myself: I am going to drink after this stranger. My lips parted, but my heart seized up while I stood there looking into the cup I held in both hands. It was not the fear of catching something that made me hesitate.

It was that other fear.

The wine in that chalice was the Blood of Christ. The blood of suffering. Zack had drunk of it, and he had validated the meaning of suffering in the fullest, human way. To participate in that Communion, that sharing of the Body and the Blood, meant more than religious symbolism. Once I had drunk, I would enter into communion with suffering at the human level.

But I had listened to his story. He was no longer a stranger to me. The word had preceded the act. Suffering — that is what is communicated by mouth.

Knowing that, I drank my share and passed the cup on.

■ ■ ■

Zachariah Rosen was born on August 19, 1953, in the Bronx, and died on July 24, 1995, in Atlanta. He had married three times, never finished high school, worked as a truck driver, found Christianity. He owned almost every movie Humphrey Bogart ever made. A poster of Albert Einstein was tacked above his bed. He loved rock 'n' roll, classic cars, and Harley-Davidson motorcycles. His Selective Service card notes the scar on his right leg where he had had cancer, and the disfigured finger on his left hand where a severed pinky, lost in a slammed door, had been reattached. He preferred printing to cursive writing and didn't like reading. Because he acquired much of his learning from what he heard, his language had an odd range to it: he knew words you wouldn't expect him to know, like "Rubenesque," but he mispronounced other words, saying "petike" for "petite." Sometimes he confused words, saying "futon" for "tofu." His roommate, Ralph Anderson, and I remember best the way Zack would say "the raft of God" for "the wrath of God."

As a Jew converted to Christianity, Zack bridged Old and New Testament views of salvation. "Jesus was very Jewish" was one of his two testimonial refrains, and this was spoken in a New Jersey accent that he never lost even though he lived in the South for many years. The other refrain: "Christ never abandoned the afflicted." Zack never completed his bar mitzvah, but his prayer shawl and yarmulke were carefully folded in plastic inside the drawer of a china cabinet. When he entered or left the house, he touched the mezuzah that was nailed to the door frame; inside the house, a picture of Jesus or a passage from Scripture hung in every room.

Zack had a terminal illness. From that moment in the church until his death a year and a half later, we were rarely apart, and I heard his story many times from different angles. Winters last long in southwest Virginia. Through two hard winters we sat huddled together on the sofa in my house, or on the sofa in his house, him talking, me listening. Before I met him, he had received a scholarship to attend Jerry Falwell's Liberty University.

Zack wanted to become a preacher. Although he attended but was not graduated from Liberty, he eventually went on to speak in churches and public schools; his testimony was broadcast over Christian radio stations and on a local Christian television show, "Ken Wright and Friends." Though I could not know for sure, I believe this preaching, and perhaps even his short education in Bible college, enabled him to organize the tripartite testimony I came to know by heart: his heritage, his affliction, his salvation.

As Zack grew weaker, I handled his correspondence, wrote out his bills, cooked for him, took him to the doctor. I sat in the room through his surgery. I fed him, helped him bathe, dressed him, tied his shoes, drove him when he couldn't drive.

"You got to write my story," he told me over and over.

He told me all the details of his life; as far as I could tell, he censored nothing.

Early on, "the book" became a common reference point between us. When people were cruel or indifferent to Zack, he told me, "Don't be upset. Put it in the book." While his ultimate recourse was God, for the moment, for the day, at the human level of existence, it was "the book," as if he wanted the book to tell the complete story of his life and death. While Zack would have believed that all things were written down in God's book and that justice fell to the hand of heaven, he was still driven by desire to have people *know* — know him, know what had happened to him.

For if you had passed him on the street, you would have thought him a street person. Sitting on a park bench, he appeared indigent, perhaps homeless, a bum. I know, because I saw him once downtown when I wasn't expecting to meet him. He sat slumped on a bench with his legs stretched out, one arm extended along the back of the bench, his face turned up to the sun. His clothes were clean but worn. His India-print shirt was faded. He looked like a man who had no place else to go.

Passers-by walked a circle around him.

■ ■ ■

When it came time to write Zack's story, I gave serious, deliberate thought to how I would write it. I told Zack I wouldn't write it unless I could write the whole story, good or bad, as I saw it. I would have to write the truth of what I saw. Zack said, "Fine. Do what you got to do."

I could not have written his story exactly the way Zack wanted because the story I saw and the story he told were different. Zack's story was about the hand of God in his life, how he had been born a Jew and had been saved by Christ. He lived his faith, and he would have liked a story entirely about God, but I saw something besides the will of God working itself out in him. I saw a story at the human level about a man struggling with the most difficult issues any human could face. This wasn't just God's story; it was Zack's. To me, his was the story of a man in search of his spiritual destiny and the horrifying consequences that attended his quest. For me, the spiritual and the human levels had to be reconciled.

Zack thought himself a man of God. He lived intensely in the Body and in the Spirit: as a man, with all the suffering, frailties, and desires of the flesh, and as a creature of God, aspiring to reach a transcendent truth about human existence grounded in his faith. Sir Thomas Browne, a seventeenth century physician, once wrote, "Thus is man that great and true amphibium whose nature is disposed to live . . . in divided and distinguished worlds . . . the one visible and the other invisible." Perhaps more acutely than most of us, Zack tried to understand the order of the invisible world by interpreting its visible signs. In his struggle to understand the significance of his spiritual destiny, he transcended the particulars of his existence and the specifics of his faith.

For me, the heart of Zack's story lay in his internal life: his relationship to God and to other human beings. I hasten to add that I do not presume to know the internal workings of his heart and his mind, and that I do not presume absolute knowledge of his spirituality. I do know what I heard and what I saw, and that is what I wrote. Because he spoke so much to me of so many things, because I spent so much time taking care of him, because we had made tapes together, because the rhythms of his language seeped into my mind, I wrote his story from his point of view. I used the "I" to speak for him. I transcribed the tapes we made. I recorded conversations he reported to me. In some places, I have reported dialogue I participated in, heard, or overheard. In other places, I have dramatized situations that Zack described. On the whole, I stitched together what I saw with what Zack and others told me. Some characters are composites. Because some persons were and are minors, and because naming names exposes individuals and institutions for better or for worse, I have fictionalized names though I rendered character as I saw it. All dates and places are noted as Zack told me. The names "Zachariah Rosen," "Ralph Anderson," and "Shelley Moffat" are fictional constructions; the persons and deeds represented by those names are not.

■ ■ ■

I did not go looking for Zack. I was not searching for a story to write. But when he entered my life, I embraced him, and *Moses Unchained* took root within the special, deep friendship we shared. As long as I knew him, he tried to make something from nothing. A simple man with simple dreams, he had a great heart and the tribulations of Job; he deserved, in my mind, to be heard. The events that happened to him are devastating; the grace with which he bore them is uplifting. He told me: "I may not have long to live but I want to spend every minute with you." In that time, he gave me the on-going gift of his life in the stories he told. *Moses Unchained* tells his story.

1 I watch the night from my front porch. Three acres behind my house, my only neighbor might still be watching television with the lights on. I see his light through naked tree branches in winter, through green foliage and yellow pollen in the spring. There's no other light in the country. Even with a full moon and a heaven full of stars, you can't see a grown man outside. You can see the light but you can't see by it. But I am glad for that. Every time I see the school bus sign across the road on the shoulder, my stomach drops, and I feel like running. The sign says "school bus stop ahead." I should call the road department one day and ask them to remove it. That sign reminds me every day. It reminds me of my step-daughter because I had them put it in for her. When Shelley came to live with me and brought the only child she had with her, a ten-year old named Gabrielle, I had the sign put up. I didn't want any speeding driver to hit my stepchild. I had married her mother honorably. I tried to give them both a respectable life. But every time I see that sign, I remember Gabrielle, and her mother and what she did to me.

■ ■ ■

One time, after I had just come off a sixteen-hour shift driving cardboard cross-country, I collapsed in front of them.

"Can't I have a little respect?" I asked. "Can't I even be the man in my own house?"

The two of them thought this was the funniest thing they ever heard. Shelley threw the dinner at me from the frying pan, hot oil still in the pan. Gabrielle walked past me, haughty, saying, "I don't have to listen to you."

I fell to the ground and held Gabrielle around the knees. "Please, please be nice to me," I begged her. She didn't say anything but called "Mama! He's *touching* me."

Shelley came running from the kitchen with an umbrella,

and she knocked me on the head with the padded length of it, screaming, "Let her go. Let her go." I squeezed Gabrielle harder, putting my face against her calves so Shelley wouldn't blind me, her beating me then on the shoulders. I released Gabrielle, me crouching on the ground, my arms folded over my face, begging Shelley, "Why can't you be nice to me? Please, please, please." Then Shelley snatched Gabrielle by the arm, and the two of them ran out the front door, taking Shelley's car to the police.

I locked the door after them, turned off all the lights in the house, and climbed into the bathtub in the downstairs bathroom. I ran hot water all over my body, hot water to clear the tears out of my eyes. The steam rose up and clouded the mirror, left a film with drops on the glossy tile. My thighs turned lobster red in the heat of it, my knees still white as my legs were bent in the tub. I sunk in the tub to my chin, wondering how my married wife turned on me so fiercely, making me, a grown man, a two hundred–pound trucker, cry on the carpet and grieve like a child for a lost pet. I wondered if there wasn't something that brought out the savage in her, like a deer laying a trail for hounds, the smell of blood so strong a dog's got no choice but to bay for the hunt. I wondered what I had done so wrong that this child, a girl of ten, then eleven, then twelve, with long, curly, light-brown hair, small blue eyes, would sneer at me with contempt when I lay crying at her feet. And then I wondered what it was in humanity that made people *turn,* like a family dog gone feral.

After an hour or more, a car pulled down my driveway, rocking its way over the ruts in the grass. Someone knocked on the front door, pounded at the back.

"This is the police," a voice said between the hammering on the door. But all the lights were out, all the doors were locked, and I was safe. No one knew for sure that I was home. So I lay down lower in the tub, sinking into warm water, letting it take the umbrella knocks out of my shoulders, listening to the police searching for me. This is what it's like to be hunted, I thought, to feel that deep fear, and yet to be invisible in the brush, concealed by six inches of lumber and dry wall, a locked door, and the law protecting me the same as it hunted me.

My thighs turned white, the steam condensed into drops that trailed back into the tub, and the bath water grew cool to the touch, making me sneeze. The telephone rang. The police left a message. "Zack Rosen. This is the sheriff's department. Turn yourself in. If you do not turn yourself in in the next twenty-four hours, there will be a warrant issued for your arrest."

I rested longer in the tepid water, now chilling instead of soothing, thinking about God and prayer, and how much I had longed for a soul mate.

My first marriage had been a disaster, so with Shelley I was committed to being married for life. Frieda, my first wife, left me with the taste of failure in my mouth. I left her after seven years of marriage. I was twenty-seven when we married, Frieda forty-two. She had had eight children by another man, all grown and out of the house. She was the dispatcher for the trucking company where we both worked, and we had lived together for three years before we got married. But one day, after we were married, I woke up and knew I couldn't spend the rest of my life with her, even though I loved her with all my heart. I was a good provider for her. She loved me, and I loved her. It was the age difference.

In between hauling loads — flowers, bread — I used to run around with some guys who drove Harleys. We worked out together, day and night. Three hours a day if I could, I built up this strong, fine body that Frieda loved. She loved my body, but when the change came — the woman's change of life — she became depressed. She sat in the kitchen, stared out the window, and cried for days at a time. She wore the same pants for a week, her hair grew stringy, needing a wash. She sat out front in an aluminum porch chair, her shoulder leaning into the webbing like it held her up. Some grief had descended upon her. Maybe she was mourning the last part of her that was young, maybe she was mourning me seeing her get old. Face to face in the mirror, did she see what I saw? Papery skin with little veins run through it. In the bed, I fell into her old flesh like drowning.

When I'd leave for a haul across the state, she made me kiss her. Squeezed up against her, my chest pressed into a bosom like my mother's, her lips pulling a kiss from my lips that stopped my breath so I'd pull away.

My face reflected in her face. The fear of losing me shone out of her eyes — that was what I saw. First, her fear. And then — I must have been a fine, precious man to inspire that much fear in a woman.

I don't say this to be bragging, but I worked out three hours a day three times a week. My thighs were huge and my ankles round as my wrist. I could press 250 pounds. I could hold my Harley, 800 pounds, like a teenager with a scooter. Frieda would say, "Oh, baby, don't look at me like that," and run out of the room, crying.

One time, when I rode my bike to the gym, Frieda came to pick me up. I came out of the gym, sweat seeping through my undershirt, dripping down my arms. She had a gun in her hand, and she stood next to the Harley. She had blown a hole in the front tire. "If you don't come home with me, I'm going to blow you away like this tire," she said. I sat in the front seat of her car with my hands resting in my lap like a schoolboy, but mentally I was packing my bags.

It was more than the age difference, it was all that fifteen years meant. Even though I left her, divorced her giving her the house, the boat, a washer and dryer, I still felt guilty about leaving her when she was old. That bitter taste of failure rose up in my throat when I thought of Shelley and Gabrielle, and it was that taste that kept me so committed to Shelley.

This time would be different. I was no longer a boy but a man in my late thirties. I married Shelley for life, me saying to myself as I buttoned up a clean shirt in the full-length mirror in our bedroom upstairs, as I combed my hair and grabbed my coat on the way to the sheriff's department to turn myself in. Whatever was wrong, we could work it out. I had left a marriage once, and it shamed me. No way I would leave this one.

"Son of a bitch," Shelley said to me when I walked into the police station.

A policeman handed me some papers of Shelley's report against me. Three pages. On green paper. How I hit her. How I hurt Gabrielle. Every kind of abuse was written against me.

Shelley crossed the room and stood next to me.

"You won't hit me now, will you, you son of a bitch, now that we are in the police station."

She smacked me across the back of the neck with the flat of her hand. "You son of a bitch," she said over and over.

Looking up at the policeman, I said nothing. Shelley was still slapping me where she could find a place, on the shoulder, on the back, while Gabrielle sat across the room, looking down at her tennis shoes, trying not to watch her mother humiliate me in public.

"The two of you better work this out," the cop said. As soon as he turned his back, Shelley wrapped her arms around my neck. "Oh, my baby. I am so afraid. It's only because I love you so much. I'm sorry, baby, I'm sorry."

By the time the policeman turned back around, Shelley was

kissing everyplace on my arm that had turned red from her slaps. She was kissing me with tears coming out of her eyes. Gabrielle was looking away even more intently, being as cold as a child could be. Shelley pulled the police report out of the cop's hand and tore it up, one page at a time, saying, "This good man could not have done all this."

I had hardly said a word, and she had changed from hell fury to arms full of love and tenderness, a sweet loving coming from her lips, her eyes soft like doe eyes, open again, as if they had been shut, to loving.

Still the two of them, they were not kind to me. Every time I see that school bus stop sign, I remember Gabrielle, and her mother, and what she did to me.

■ ■ ■

Before I bought this house, a policeman lived here with his new wife and a crazy daughter. The daughter must have been crazy because she painted all the walls black. The ceiling black too. She laid down a blood-red carpet on the floor, and all the windows were sealed up with aluminum foil taped to the sills with masking tape. The day I came to buy the house, I saw that daughter. She had white-white makeup on her face. Her hair was black as pitch, and she wore red lipstick smeared over her mouth, so much that the lipstick mouth was bigger than her real mouth, a clown mouth but more like a mouth of hell outlined in fire-engine red. She had long fingernails too, long red ones. Maybe she was sixteen. Maybe a little younger or a little older. But she was so skinny and so strange, she scared me. That room scared me too, like it was a place for a vampire to live, or some other force of evil. No place for a young girl, but this wasn't a young girl in her heart. Her heart had something old and evil in it, cankered up like rotting wood. That was her room, that black-walled, red-carpeted room, which was good in that it was one of four bedrooms, but it wasn't a good room for Gabrielle, who was ten with light-brown hair, kind of wavy like it was too curly, and little blue eyes, and white skin. Gabrielle was chubby, and she wore big shirts or big sweaters, like fat girls do. She never was kind to me, but it didn't have to do with anything about my being a stepdad.

That white-faced, red-lipped vampire girl scared me so bad I hardly stayed long enough to sign the papers. And I am a big man. When I had my health, I weighed 210 pounds, stood six feet tall without my steel-toed boots. I had so many muscles people used to say I looked like Jethro in the "Beverly Hillbillies."

In Roanoke, Virginia, I delivered number two fuel to the railroad line. Number two fuel is for furnaces or for diesel, and my tanker carried nine thousand gallons though I never drove with more than seventy-five hundred. Nobody would. At the railroad line, I pumped the fuel into the tank on the train using thirty-foot long hoses four inches in diameter; they were called "four-inch" hoses. When I pumped oil, each hose weighed a hundred pounds. I could handle two — one over each shoulder, a nozzle in each hand. I could hold those hoses hour after hour. Other fellows would kid me about my endurance. It was something I got into, hauling that fuel around.

One time when I was hauling fuel, I found the hatch on the fuel tank on the railroad car was closed. I climbed up on the catwalk, maybe thirty feet off the ground, and was making my way across the catwalk, hand over hand, when something strange happened. My hand went limp. It lost all feeling. It lost all power. My hand gave in. I fell. Landed on the concrete thirty feet down.

Hurt like a son of a bitch.

Before I met Shelley, I hauled flowers out of Florida to New

York in a refrigerator truck. We carried long-stemmed roses on their way north. They would go to invalids in hospitals or to mothers on their birthdays. Maybe a rose would see a fancy bud vase in a restaurant with pink tablecloths. That Florida–New York haul was a two-day trip, and I was sharing the driving with my buddy named George. George was ten years older than me — him about forty-five, with a pot that hung over his belt like he had a snake wrapped around his waist under his shirt. He smoked like a chimney, had that yellow face of bad circulation, pink eyes from smoke. In South Carolina, George was driving and I was nodding off when he said, "Feel like pulling over?"

I nodded my head, not so much as "yes" or "no" but to show him that I heard. He eased off slowly down the ramp to a little place that looked like a regular Union 76 truck stop; but it was not a Union 76, it was a building with a sign that said in pea-green neon light "Peaches Galore." By then it was after midnight, and three other rigs were parked in the lot.

George pulled a greasy comb out from behind the seat and ran it through his hair. A cloud of cigarette smoke matted his shirt, and when he combed through his hair, his shirt material moved and a cloud of smoke came off him. I could hardly stand to be in the cab with him except that I kept my window cracked.

We went inside, took a booth near the cash register, and waited for the waitress. "Jackie" — the name on her pin — was a waitress in a pink tank top and pink hot pants, yellow hair piled high on top of her head with the ends of black bobby pins sticking out. Jackie laid a menu down in front of us, and she laid it down bending over, not dropping it onto the place setting. George opened the menu, looked at the door to the kitchen, closed the menu, and told me: "You go ahead and order." Then he got up, stabbing his hand in the back of his pants to tuck in his shirt, which wouldn't stay tucked in because of his stomach.

I flipped through the selections, the specials. They had hamburgers reasonably priced. When the waitress came back — a different one in black hot pants and "Meg" fastened on her bra strap — she asked me, "What'll you have, handsome?"

I said, "Hamburger. Fries. Mayo. No onion. Give me a coffee, too, to go."

"Anything else?" she asked. She rested her menu on her hip. She nodded at the door to the kitchen, and asked, "Where'd your friend go?"

"Nothing else," I said.

All the truckers knew it was a hooking stop. All of them but me, though I had heard about it. Once I saw that Meg was waiting on my order, swinging her hip side to side and smiling at me, I knew where George had gone.

The smell of sizzling beef filled the room so full that I could almost hear it cooking, while George was humping a waitress in a back room. I thought to myself, "Here I am smelling my dinner while George is fucking." It made me feel I ought to be doing something more notable then smelling my meat on the grill, looking around a room with stale air and lights that bleach the life out of everything, looking at the plastic plants hung in the corners in front of the window. I wondered how a man could fuck in the time it took to fry a hamburger.

Meg brought out my hamburger — twenty thin slivers of fries on the side, the sesame bun held in a place by a toothpick with red frills speared through the pickle chip — and set it down in front of me. I turned the ketchup upside down, then shook it before I took off the cap.

"Anything else, sweetness?" she asked me.

I asked her about the coffee.

She said, "Sweetness, I would do you for nothing."

But then she brought me my coffee.

"I'm hauling roses," I told her.

George went to the back of the rig and got a bouquet of roses from the load, then waved at me as I sat in the front sipping my hot black coffee. I imagine he must have given that bouquet to Jackie. Happy at the little romance he brought to Peaches Galore, Jackie gave him some pie in a Styrofoam container to bring back to the cab. "She give me two pieces," he said, setting the brown paper bag on the driver's seat as he hauled his ass into the cab. "One's for you," he said, turning the ignition to warm up that engine, turning on the lights.

I was thirty-six years old at the time, divorced from Frieda, always halfway looking for work. I was built like a farm animal, but my soul was saved by the Lord. I was so handsome a hooker would call me "sweetness" and give me some goody for free.

But it was clear that the hand of God was on me. Even when I was a boy growing up in New Jersey, my mother said, "Everyone could tell you loved the Lord."

I believed God had marked me out for something special. I knew this for sure because the Lord had sent me a vision.

I was seventeen, coming back from my job as a waiter on a rainy day. The sky was black, everything was dark. My heart was sad with longing because I was lonely. I listened to Scripture on the radio, and right before I turned it off, I heard the preacher say, "God speaks to the Jews through thunder and lightning." I got out of the car.

All of a sudden, a huge black cloud appeared in the sky. I didn't see it but felt as if a shadow passed over me. Halfway up the walk, I was paralyzed. Literally paralyzed. My legs wouldn't work. My arms froze in place. My head was welded to my neck. I heard a voice say, "Look up. Look up." I looked up and saw that thunder cloud. A voice from nowhere said, "Faith. Prayer."

Then my legs came back. My knees unlocked. My arms could work. I knew I had received a special vision from the Lord. My life would be dedicated to His work. When Moses took a census of the people of Israel to collect young men to go to war in Israel, the Lord said that Moses should not count the men of the tribe of Levi. They were exempted from this counting because God gave them a special function. God told Moses, "Thou shalt appoint the Levites over the tabernacle of testimony." I remembered that: the Levites were in charge of testimony. Moses himself was the son of a man and a woman of Levi. That was like me, the son of a man and a woman of Levi. Me and Moses, related. And the Lord had given me a vision. Which I did not ask for. Which I did not know how to interpret at the time. You know, it's stronger than the IRS or the army when the Lord has something for you to do. That was why, at Peaches Galore, the only piece I ever had was that piece of pie.

■ ■ ■

One night when I was driving truck, while Shelley was still alive, something strange happened to me. It was so strange that for a time I thought it was a dream. I thought it was a dream until I pulled into a truck stop down the road near Sarasota.

A bunch of truckers was sitting around talking about picking up hitchhikers. Waiting for my coffee, I said I never picked up hitchhikers because if you got a girl in the cab and something happened you'd be up for a law suit. Some guy said he picked up a naked girl who had been raped and left for dead in the Everglades. A shiver ran up my back. Because, as I told you, what I saw was like a dream.

I was driving truck for the Quality Bakery on the east coast. There were no bakeries on the west coast of Florida then, so the Quality plant sent out loads to west Florida. My truck held thirty racks of bread and cake, and each rack contained about three hundred loaves of bread. Quality Bakery turned out fifteen full truckloads a day. I was hauling a load on a road between Arcadia and Sarasota, driving through the Everglades. It was spooky. The swamp was threatening — skinny tree branches splintered like they'd been struck with lightning, low scrub on both sides of the road, rattlers in the palmetto scrub, alligators in the swamp.

I was tired then, driving with both hands squeezed around the wheel. The heater filled the cab with warm air that dried out my eyes, and I blinked to raise the tears that would wet them. On nights like that, you need tears to keep your eyes focused. You drive by following the yellow line in the middle; that line fills up your whole eye, like it is connected at one end to the road and one end to your brain, and, as you look, you keep your eyes on the line to keep the rig straight. But you know that off to the side in a dark blur, on a cold night, evil things lurk in the edges of the world, in the dark blurred edges of the world. You can't look aside because if you did your hand would take you where your eyes looked, and the rig would overturn. That is the story of Lot's wife. Sodom and Gomorrah burn up on every side. People are screaming, their clothes on fire. The sky touches the earth, and God sends angels or devils out of black thunderheads to torch the world, and your only task is to look straight. You know something happens on the borders. But you keep looking straight ahead.

I was praying in my mind or praying out loud, singing hymns, trying to make a noise to keep my mind alive, when, all of a sudden, a white body ran out of the brush, came running down the road toward my truck. *Night of the Living Dead,* I thought, remembering those images of bodies running toward the living people. I was so scared.

It was a woman. She was running at me, naked except for her underwear. Her long blond hair fanned out as she ran. I couldn't believe that there was a living soul out there in the cold. It wasn't weather any person would be out in, being dead winter and after midnight. Nothing human would be out on such a night. A ghost. That body was so naked and so white. I pulled down on the trolley brake, like a blinker stick on the right of the steering wheel. I stepped on the brake pedal that worked the rig and the fourteen wheels on the load. I lay on those two sets of brakes so fast that my brakes locked. Fourteen drums catching on the inside of the rim. Fourteen squealing tires turning against the resistance of the drum. The woman running into the brights, catching the light in her eyes, making her eyes gleam red, running toward me, some mad deer hungry for light. But the rig kept moving on and on, a truck doesn't stop like a car, and now me sliding on the pavement, her on the side of the road raising up her hands, me sliding past her, looking out the window, seeing this white, ghost mouth open wide, calling me. Calling for help.

Screaming.

Ralph has been smoking outside again. There's a couple of butts on the crushed rock, little white butts of cancer sticks I tell him. Ralph came to live with me after Shelley went. He needed a place to live because he was divorcing his wife of twenty years, Marianne. I get so mad at him for smoking. He was miraculously cured of cancer, and now he flaunts the Lord by smoking. What does he think? He'll get a miracle twice? He still wears special socks, like support hose, when he goes into work, carpentering. He's on his feet all day. It has something to do with the way they stripped all the lymph nodes out of his legs and groin. He was diagnosed with stage-five melanoma. The doctors told him to go home and put his affairs in order even though they were going to try surgery. They stripped twenty-six lymph nodes from his groin to his knee. Then the doctors were going to operate again to check if the cancer had come back, but the second time around they found nothing.

Ralph prayed every day. He had a special passage from Scripture, Psalm 103. He read, "Bless the Lord, my soul . . . Who forgiveth thine iniquities, who healeth all diseases." When the doctors opened him up again, there was nothing but human flesh and tissue. No cancer. One day he had cancer; the next day he didn't. He found his power in the psalm, in "healeth all diseases." I've seen the medical file. The Lord sure loved him.

Ralph lives in the Harley room, which was once my stepson's room, which was once Shelley's book room. It's on the corridor connecting the laundry room, the downstairs bathroom (Ralph's more or less), and the kitchen. The white room where Ralph grows things is located directly above his bedroom room, and nobody's in that room now, so he has privacy. This house is a two-story house with white columns that go from the front porch to the roof. Coming off Parkway, you go down the road about a mile, come around and down the bend, and that white house jumps into your face at the bottom of the valley. The living room downstairs is where I keep my speakers, my VCR, and my fish tank. There's nothing much in the dining room but a dining room table where I fold my clothes when I take them out of the dryer. I can't go up the stairs any more, so now I dress in the dining room.

In winter, I lean against the brick chimney that makes part of the wall between the dining room and the kitchen. Upstairs the chimney passes through the master bedroom where there is a Jacuzzi; Ralph put it in. Upstairs, too, the red room from the policeman's crazy daughter. Nowadays, I don't spend too much time upstairs. The steps are hard on my legs. My knees creak when they catch, or sometimes they catch late, and I snap my fingers around the bannister like they were a vise. Sometimes my legs stop working, like when I was on the catwalk. Sometimes I can't walk, the dizziness is so bad. Sometimes I can't even open my eyes, the room spins around me while I'm lying on the sofa.

All that, from Shelley too.

Sometimes I stand at the foot of the stairs, ready to climb with my hand on the bannister that Ralph put in, and I look up, the upstairs lit with the daylight light coming through the windows upstairs. It looks like a church window on a Hallmark card for a wedding. I don't even want to go up there any more. It is a sign of how much my life has shrunk. From hauling roses up and down the East Coast, to my two acres, to my house, to my sofa. Not even the upstairs of my own house is a place I can go.

Ralph used to be a deacon in the Rainbow Baptist Church. He taught children about the Lord in Sunday school and in Bible camp. He taught his own three children about the Lord, and his wife, Marianne, was a pious woman. When Ralph left the church, he stopped reading and praying. He smoked like he was going to live forever. He let his hair grow out. It's past his shoulders now, long black hair with silver streaks in it. He has a pointed beard, and a thin, narrow face with black eyes alive like an animal lived in them. Marianne hates me now. She thinks Ralph became like this because of me. She says, "That Zack, he helped Ralph break his vows."

I only gave him the downstairs room to live in after he left. When my money ran short, I started asking him for rent after a year. He helps me with fixing up the house and the shed. He has a tractor, which I need to mow the two acres of yard. The grass gets so high in the back, it's like a jungle. Even if the deer came down from the mountain to eat the apples from my tree, you might not be able to see them for the tall grass.

When I go into the kitchen for something to eat, Ralph is

standing at the stove making blintzes. He wears a towel tucked in around the waist of his jeans to make an apron, and he flips the blintzes up and down.

"I already got the mail," he says, nodding to the kitchen table. "You got a new CD. The Moody Blues."

"You been smoking too much, Ralph," I tell him.

"Put it on the list. 'Stop smoking.'"

He nods to the list, "Things for Ralph to do," taped to the side of refrigerator.

Things for Ralph to do: Paint the peak of the house. Retile the blue bathroom. Mow the yard.

He does things for me because I hardly charge him any rent. He's two weeks behind anyway.

"Seriously, Ralph," I say.

"You remind me of Marianne sometimes. Do this. Do this. Don't do this. I feel like we're married. You want some blintzes?"

He flips them onto a plate. I turn on the CD player in the next room. I got fourteen speakers hooked up so I can play the music as loud as I like. What's the point of living in the country if you can't play music in your own darn house?

Ralph's boots leave little black marks on the linoleum, and he makes a trail to the kitchen table. He pours honey on his blintzes, and some drops fall on the floor. I'm not very hungry, so I just stir them around on my plate.

Ralph says, while he's eating, "We got some trouble, Zack."

"Marianne wants to move in?"

"Worse than that. Eat a'ready. We got problems of the serious kind. A groundhog."

"Where?"

"Where? Are you kidding? Everywhere. In the yard. Out in the field. Holes. Everywhere you look. Holes. Back by the Harley. We got to do something about that groundhog, Zack."

"Blintzes, and again blintzes. I wish you'd learn how to cook something besides blintzes. Cheese blintzes. Peanut butter."

Ralph says, "This house needs a woman."

"We got the appliances," I tell him. "If we just had a woman to run them."

"Maybe if we went to the road and lined up all the appliances — you think we could get a woman in this house if you showed the appliances? A juicer. A dishwasher. A food processor. A blender. These blintzes taste like shit. The bee man called. He's got some more capsules for you. I want to get rid of that groundhog. It's killing the yard. Can you believe it, Marianne called. She wants me to come over and fix the roof. She still doesn't believe it. She still thinks I'm coming back to fix the roof. Zack, we got to waste that groundhog."

Ralph tosses his dishes into the sink. He wants to shoot it before he goes to work on Patrice's house for the day. She is his boss at B&B and he has been helping her build a house. The two of them work together, out there by Smith Mountain Lake, day in and day out, hammering planks, cutting drywall.

He goes to the closet where he keeps his gun, puts on a camouflage jacket and his biker sunglasses.

"You look like ZZ Top," I tell him, him holding his gun over his shoulder like a kid with a popgun. He shakes his hair on his shoulders to agree.

"Before you waste it, Ralph, answer me this."

"Yeah?"

"What is the purpose of the groundhog to the Creation?"

All those years driving truck, I listened to preaching on the Christian radio network. When I stopped for coffee, even at a place like Peaches Galore, I brought the Word with me.

It was a testimony to Jesus that I, a Jew, of the Leviticus tribe, a direct descendant of the tribe of Moses, had come to the Lord. My conversion gave the strongest testimony to the power of Christ, because the Way must be the right if someone from the oldest of the religions came to Christ. Churches loved me. There was something extra authentic about a converted Jew. Besides, I was a direct descendant of Moses.

Mabel, my mother, was the only Jewish woman to move into the Polish Catholic neighborhood in Hackensack, New Jersey. My foster brothers, Bill and Bob, still remember her by the yellow Cadillac Eldorado she drove there without a husband but with three sons, me the oldest. My brothers, Frankie and Murray, had green eyes and light-colored hair. I was the only one of them colored like my father, with dark eyes and hair. My mother raised all the children herself, cooking in a restaurant until she opened her own truck stop and had enough money for good things. Eventually I began to work in the restaurant. My arms and chest grew huge from moving around the extra large cans of tomatoes. That was when I started to get big. But even though I was big at sixteen, smart-alecky but strong, she beat me all the time with a wooden spoon. One time she broke the spoon on my head and then beat me again for breaking the spoon.

Many years later, she told me, "You don't know what to do with the first one."

Even today, my brothers turn their eyes away from me when I say anything about our childhood. We had two different childhoods. In theirs, I was the oldest brother who was always in trouble — drinking, drugging, working on cars, till I flunked out of the tenth grade. When I was seventeen, I owned a Cadillac Eureka hearse that I used to cruise the main street in Hackensack. A cop broke up a pot party I was holding in the hearse in front of a Dunkin' Donuts. I wasn't very smart; Ralph says I must have wanted to get caught.

Anyway, my mother beat me so much with the wooden spoon that the neighbors heard me scream.

Mrs. V., in the brownstone next to ours, called the child welfare agency. They took my mother to court before they took me away from her. Mrs. V. raised me as hers, with her two boys, Bill and Bob, since Mrs. V. was a good Catholic woman. She raised me next door to my mother.

"Who does he think he is?" Mabel would ask, when she saw me from across the street, me working on one of my cars, "Moses unchained?"

When I was a grown man, I went to the library looking for pictures of Moses.

My father, Sal, comes from Greek, Italian, and Spanish roots. Of the twelve tribes of Abraham, he belongs to the tribe of Levi. He is a Leviticus Jew but he is as nutty as a fruitcake — in and out of mental hospitals for what is now called manic depression, on full-time disability the rest of the time because the only thing he could keep track of was numbers. This is how my father would talk, not in the exact method, but in the sound of his counting: "Zack, you were born on August 19, 1953. That was the same day the Madison Square Garden served popcorn at boxing matches, the *New York Times* increased the circulation to three million readers, and Winston Churchill started to paint roses with oil on canvas." Sal is still a genius at numbers. Birth dates, social security numbers, car registration numbers — he can calculate anything with them.

As a young man he had a full head of hair, a mouth full of charm, and playful, wicked eyes that used to drive the ladies crazy when he looked over a bouquet of roses to tell them all the significant events that happened on their birth number. He counted other women's dates through the birth of my youngest brother, Frankie, while he was sleeping in their beds, stirring cream into their coffee, and turning their phone numbers into a code that had meaning in history. Even when he was seventy-five, he still complained about the woman chasing after him, that Doris who wouldn't stop talking and always wanted him even though she slept with *the bag*. That Doris was born on the same day as Pearl Harbor, I knew what that meant, didn't I?

My mother kicked the old man out when Frankie was two months old.

My family did not know the Lord Jesus Christ. But I did.

4 My whole life I had trouble with women. I couldn't keep them off me. My mother used to tell me, "Zack, you are so handsome. Why don't you shave your face so people can see it?" I couldn't help it. Even last week, my teacher friend Frances took me to the grocery store. I was sitting down at the deli counter having a Coke. I felt eyes on me. When I looked up, I saw a strange woman staring at me down the aisle, staring at me like she was interested. Maybe it's rare to see a good-looking, forty-year-old man relaxing in the grocery store in the middle of the day, but it's still rude to stare.

Just what I always needed, more women.

Ralph saying, "Zack, you got so many appliances."

While I was living in Jupiter Beach, Florida, after being divorced from Frieda, I started to get back pain. I had an accident that damaged my back. I used to have to unload huge racks of bread, push them off the back of the truck, and push those racks into the bakeries or stores. I could hardly sit down and drive, the pain racked my body so bad. To keep me from putting in for workman's compensation, the company sent me for a month to a pain clinic in Miami. My back pain was so bad, I could hardly move.

The first week there, I lay in a hospital bed with a white sheet pulled over me, groaning from the pain. The first day, the pain doctor came to visit me, Dr. Mary Dolor. She had skinny legs below a short skirt. The hem hung down only about an inch below her white coat. Her black hair was twisted in a knot pinned to her head, and she had black eyes and a thin face. She wrote things down on a clipboard as she asked me questions about my medical history. When I told her, she wrote the answers down, but she was looking without looking at me.

"Heart disease?" she asked.

"No." She wrote that down.

"Cancer?"

"Yes ma'am. In my right leg. It was cut out when I was a boy."

I still have the scar, a raised white line down my ankle that goes into my shoe. It looks like the dotted part that comes with my CD orders, where it says "Tear off at the perforation."

"Arthritis?"

"No."

"On any medication?"

"No, ma'am."

"Anything else?"

"No."

Before I noticed it, she lifted up the white sheet and was looking at me naked under the sheet. She acted like it was a medical examination. She felt my leg that had the cancer, ran a finger along the scar line, but it did not feel like a doctor's touch. It felt like a touching of discovery. But not discovering my reflexes at the muscular level.

"I can't move," I told her.

She came back every day even though I started the pain treatments. The other people at the clinic were elderly, suffering with untreatable pain, some from arthritis. In my Jazzercise class, older ladies in track suits swung their arms back and forth. I was the only man in the class, and the women used to be on me like pea hens. I was their pet.

By the end of the week, Dr. Mary Dolor had left me the key to her house, and I spent most of the nights there. Because, by the second day there in the hospital, she called me into her office and shut the door.

She pulled up that short skirt, showing her black garter belt and hose, did a little striptease, and then did me. After a while, she'd do me coming and going, inside and out. The fucking was so easy, came so natural to me, that I didn't have to try or anything. She was the first woman I made love to after Frieda, and my body wanted it so bad. Not to mention that the pain turned my body into something extra sensitive. While my back would be screaming, sending messages to my brain that spelled out fire and sharp pricks, my penis sent my brain the exact opposite message, and the sex that blew the top off my head nearly left me crippled the next morning. I liked it with Dr. Mary Dolor, her giving me the house key, her steady screwing, her love of that striptease, that power thing of the doctor, us playing doctor, so that we got to the point of replaying my first day, with me lying in the bed naked, pretending I couldn't move. Her playing "Let the doctor fix it." Then her climbing on top of me, her in her office uniform without any underwear on.

Even with a bad back, I could function like a man.

At the end of a month, though I still felt shooting, hot pain in my back, I got my walking papers. I had been through the whole program, swung my hips in rhythm in Jazzercise. I thought, since I would be leaving, that it would be time for me to get serious about Dr. Mary Dolor. On that last day, when I packed my bag and went into the office, I was going to ask her to come back to Jupiter Beach with me. I could go back to trucking. She was a doctor and could find work. She wouldn't have to stay in Miami. I created an entire life for us. This life was built on us being together, on us playing doctor within the bonds of honorable matrimony. We could do this thing forever, it made me so happy, and we wouldn't have to sneak about it.

Before I could say anything to her in her office about the plans I hoped we would share, she shook my hand good-bye, gave me her card, and wished me well. It was the fastest brush off I had ever seen. And I had been to her house almost every day for a month. I was stunned.

In Jupiter Beach, I still had back pain, and I couldn't shake it. Maybe it was the pain of something else, some kind of longing for a love that would be complete, a love that could heal all the wounds. Jesus gave me that kind of love, but I needed more of the human kind. Human touch is healing touch. I longed for it. I prayed to Jesus to send me my soul mate, my *b'sherta*, the Jews call it. For though I was converted to Christianity, I had been raised with Jewish ways: Jews believe that a man needs a woman and a woman needs a man, that no human is complete alone. Someone existed in the world for me, and I prayed to meet that person.

Then I prayed more that I would know her when I met her. "Give me a sign, Lord, give me a sign." I prayed in the morning and the evening, made my life a prayer. Sometimes I thought that Dr. Mary Dolor, the pain doctor, had been the cause of a punishment, that God was punishing me by delay, by the empty nights that filled my ears with ringing, with the drumming of my own heart driving me out of the little house I rented, into the night, looking for my soul mate.

Because my back still hurt me so I couldn't drive, Quality Bakery laid me off. I got an attorney to bring a suit against them, and, while I was waiting for the case, I prayed and found a job in a gas station pumping gas for $5 an hour.

I had my Harley at the time and used to take it into the shop just to talk about motorcycles. It was the same bike that Frieda had shot up. Even though I didn't have any money, I went to the shop to check on some speakers so I could listen to rock 'n' roll on the radio. Sateen Rogers, an old Monterey biker, worked there, and him and me used to talk about bikes, sit together over a table, taking turns turning the pages to see the new models. Sateen said to me one afternoon, "You know the Lord, don't you, Zack?"

I said I did.

"I found this church," he said. "They got great music. Gospel music. Lifts the lead out of your heart."

I said I would go sometime. And that I would come back once my legal settlement was in, and then I would order some speakers and maybe do some other things to cherry-out the bike.

There was no way to work on the bike till then. My back was hurting so much that I needed to lay down a lot. There wasn't much traffic at this station, so I'd go in my truck and lie down to rest my back. When I heard the bell ring, I got up from the seat to pump gas. One day my boss discovered my practice and fired my ass for laziness.

Sometimes in the night, I'd call Mary Dolor because I wanted to tell her about my pain. It felt like hot pinpricks sticking into my back or a sharp cutting when I leaned or stood up too long. But that pain covered a deeper pain. And Dr. Dolor did not return any calls.

Truckers don't have much of a life. They drive all day. Go home. Go to bed. Your bones still shake for hours after you get out of the truck. How is anyone driving truck going to meet a woman? The driving takes odd hours, and when you're awake half the world is asleep, and who wants to go to a bar when you could sleep in your own bed?

My mother never met my first wife. Meanwhile, my brothers were growing like straight grass in the sun, going to college, getting jobs. They were working hard in ways I never could because I would fall into the dent of an invisible wound, reeling, holding my head like I was a blind man. "Lord, Lord," I cried at night. I was still waiting for my destiny, and my heart was breaking from the aloneness of my life.

The sound of an engine became the only sound that could fill up my heart, the only sound to quiet the steady drumming at night before I slept. I rode my bike frequently then, rode in traffic in the night along the Florida turnpikes, rode in the day, rode in the rain like a character in a storybook. There is a story — I don't remember where I heard it — where a man rides his horse to get somewhere fast. He has to get a doctor for his son, and he rides through dark woods. The branches whip his face. The wind blows the horse's mane into his face, stinging his eyes. When he cries, he cries blood. But he urges the horse on further and further, drives his heels into its sides, whips its legs with a switch.

The harder he pounds, the fiercer the rain comes, and urgency whips him into whipping the horse. All he knows is the need to find the doctor. Death is the dog barking at the horse's heels. Death chases the horse, wanting to hamstring it, wants to devour the father, but he reaches around with his whip and smacks death across the face. Death slows down, howling with pain, a paw raised to its snout, whining. Then the dog redoubles its efforts, doubles its tread, jumps with leaps and bounds. And always the man rides with death at his heels.

I ran from loneliness like it was death in that story. Filled my ears with motor, breathed exhaust like it gave me life. The vibrating of a road under wheels drives the pain out of your bones, fills up your heart with drumming. I used to ride the Harley in the morning, in the evening, at night, fully done up in my leathers though it was Florida.

So it was on a Sunday morning that I was driving down this Florida road when I heard the sound of gospel music. Joyous music that cut through the wind on the bike, that came over the roar of the Harley engine. The music came from a white-washed cinder-block building with a cross over the door. I pulled into the grass, low saw grass with sandspurs, and parked my bike in the oyster-shell lot. I unzipped my jacket, pulled off my helmet, and rested on the seat in the shade of a palm tree listening to the joy of the Lord in that music. I shut my eyes to let it fill me on the inside.

A voice called, "Is that you, Zack Rosen?"

It was Sateen Rogers, standing at the door, shutting the door behind him. From the wooden steps, he called, "Come in, Zack. This is the church."

"I'm in my leathers, Sateen," I told him. "I can't come in."

"The Lord don't care how you're dressed," he said.

"But I do," I said, thinking it disrespectful to enter the Lord's house dressed up like a Hell's Angel with steel-toed boots, a mustache, and black leather.

"I'll listen from the outside," I told him and waved as he went back into the church.

But next Sunday I was there in black pants and a nice white shirt. Long sleeved. I had tattoos on both arms. Biker blue. A man shouldn't show his tattoos in church. Even though God sees them anyway.

Jewish people always look for a sign. They always want to see the visible. When I walked in the church the first time, what I saw on the podium was a banner with the Star of David in the middle and on top "Jerusalem"; on the bottom it said "Israel." I said to myself, "No one here knows I am Jewish. There is a reason why I am here." I didn't know at the time, but the pastor of that church was in Israel, praying for Jews to come into his church. I heard that later.

Then the preacher came to pulpit, a thin, balding man in a gray suit with a blue tie. The black-rimmed glasses he wore made his face look frail, like his skull would crush if you touched him up the side of the head with a book.

About halfway through the service, a woman sitting in front of me started to make strange noises. She shook her shoulders around, and whatever she was saying seemed to be exciting for her. I thought, "That's not Hebrew." I didn't know what transpired. When another person spoke, I thought, "Look at this. Long distance messages." I didn't understand anything about speaking in tongues. But now that I have knowledge of God about speaking in tongues, I understand that a person who speaks in tongues has to be able to interpret it, and it has to do with nothing more than to glorify God. That was the first time I had ever heard it.

Meanwhile, the preacher was saying, "Put your faith in Jesus, and you will be healed. He will make a way where there is no way. All you have to do is knock. For it is written, 'Knock and the door shall be opened.' There's healing going on right now. Right this minute. The Spirit is telling me that someone right now is feeling the Spirit in him. Who is it? Come up here and speak. Does anyone want to come up here and speak?"

I was sitting in the pew, taken over by the welcome that the banner spoke to me. This was a church that wanted Jews for the Lord, and that is exactly what I was, a Jew and a Christian. But moreover, when he said the word "healing," my muscle jumped in my leg. It was my cancer leg.

A lady was sitting a couple of pews in front of me. I couldn't see her from the front, but she had long blond hair in a braid that reached down to the middle of the pew. You could tell she was maybe fifty by the hair, old hair looking different from young hair no matter what the color. She started to rise, answering to the preacher's call about a testimony to a healing.

But before she could get up fully, the preacher raised his hand palm out. "Wait a minute. There's someone else here who has something to say."

I knew the Holy Spirit must have said something to him, knowing about the jump in my ankle. So I stood up and went to the front of the church. It was the first time since the sixth grade I had got up in front of people. And then, never before more than three people.

"Up here?" I asked the preacher, me starting on the stair for the pulpit. He said, "No. Stay where you are. That's fine."

I was supposed to give my testimony about my healing. So I said, "My name is Zachariah Rosen. I am a direct descendant of Moses from the tribe of Levi. I am a full-blooded Levite. And I have been saved. I accepted Christ when I was seventeen. I have never spoke in front of anybody before. I have a real bad back. I been in the hospital for a month with this back. I had problems with my right leg on and off all my life. Had cancer in that leg when I was boy. When the pastor said the word 'heal,' I had a sensation in that leg. My leg jumped. That's all I wanted to say."

While I was still standing up front, looking at all those people looking at me, I felt quivery but alive.

The preacher said, "Alleluia. In Jesus's name. Got anything else you want to say?"

I said, "I am a Jew. But I'm saved. I come from good family. Everyone in my family is a corporate executive. My mother is an Ashkenazic Jew, and my father is a Sephardic Jew. My grandfather passed away; his name was Saul. He was born in Ephesus in what's now called Turkey. It doesn't matter what you got if you don't know the Lord. Jesus was very Jewish."

At the end of church I wanted to run out, thinking maybe I had said too much. Sateen, who had been sitting behind me, grabbed my sleeve before I was out the door, his bony fingers making creases in the cloth. He slapped me on the shoulder blade with his other hand, saying, "I'm glad you came, Zack. Stick around to meet the preacher."

Then he guided me outside and waited with me, his one hand still against my shoulder blade, holding me in place with a magnetism of touch. I didn't know if I was supposed to keep talking to him, or not say anything. We waited for people to come out so Sateen could shake their hands and say, "Amen."

People came by to shake my hand.

"Glad to have you with us, brother."

"Bless the Lord. Give me your hand. Wonders and miracles."

"If a Jew can come to Jesus, anybody can."

The preacher came to me, with the wind blowing his tie up, but he smoothed it down, and shaking my hand told me, "Pastor

Johnson is in Israel right this minute. He wants to bring the Jewish people to the Lord."

"Praise the Lord," I said.

I felt like a celebrity with all those holy people coming to thank me. Good Christian folk, family people. A woman came up the aisle toward me, a small woman with brown hair and wearing a blue dress with stockings and sandals. While Sateen was talking in my one ear about a gospel band, this woman slipped up to my other side. Even with heels on, she came only to the middle of my chest. She touched my arm so lightly, it felt soft as sunshine. Or maybe an angel.

She said, "I want you to know that you are not alone. I am also a Leviticus Jew. I am glad to see that you are following God."

Then she let go of my arm and slipped down the stairs.

At that point my whole life would change. It can't be reversed. You can't unring the bell.

All I thought about was getting back to this woman.

I watched her walk through the parking lot. Her skirt whipped around her calves as she opened the door and eased herself into the front seat of a white Camry. I pulled away from Sateen, saying, "I got to go," and I ran down the stairs, down the concrete path, across the parking lot. Before she could pull out, I stepped in front of her car, waving her down. She pulled around so I was near her front window, and she rolled down the window.

"Excuse me, Miss," I said to her through the window. "Can I talk to you a minute?"

She raised her dark gray eyes at me. For the first time in my life, looking into her eyes, I saw my face inside of her face. When we finally started speaking, I knew within five minutes that I had found my soul mate, my *b'sherta*.

She gave me her phone number. She wrote it down on an old deposit slip she pulled from the back of her checkbook.

I was in Florida, Jensen Beach. I was born in the Bronx, grew up in Manhattan at the age of nine. This woman was Shelley Sondheim Moffat. She was from the same county as me in New Jersey. She was in the same church as me on that day. I was overwhelmed at finding a Leviticus Jewish woman from the same place where I grew up, thirteen hundred miles from my home in New Jersey, in a Baptist church. The chances of that are less than finding a needle in a haystack.

The woman had my face. My heritage. My belief in God. My interests. I knew in less than five minutes that I was going to marry her. I knew I had found my soul mate.

I had prayed faithfully for almost two and a half years that God would send her to me, and that I would know without a doubt that that *was* the woman. How much more proof could I have? What was I expecting — a notarized statement from God?

All the signs were there.

Ralph knows I love the desert. After I set up the fish tank, he brought me a background scene to set in the back of the fish. The Grand Canyon is wrapped around four sides of the octagonal tank, and the gravel at the bottom of the tank is hot pink. The walls of the canyon are pink, and a red dawn ripples behind the bubbled-up current. The air bubbles come out of the lid of a treasure chest at the bottom; the top rises and falls with the beats of the air. Against the canyon wall, a few mules trot up the path. The black-and-white zebra fish look like a part of the scene, look like they are swimming between the mules.

It's dawn at the Grand Canyon and at the house. The zebra fish are picking at the largest one in the school. Most of the zebras travel back and forth up and down the current, sometimes dipping near the bottom, sometimes flying over its edge like birds, but the largest of the zebras hangs back, then moves to the bottom of the tank and wobbles in the gravel.

Ralph and me sit in front of the tank, watching the fish travel to the north rim.

"Look at them," Ralph says, pointing to the tank with the smoking end of his cigarette. "Fish have special radar."

As the large zebra wobbles, the others come around it and nip at its fins. Already, it's got a red place on its body like a bruise. Any other day, the zebra would nip back and chase the others. Now it falls over with every nip, like one of those kid's balloon punching bags with the feet fixed into the floor. It flops over and rights itself. Flops over again.

"They can tell when one is sick," Ralph says.

"You think so, Ralph?"

"Sure. Just look at them. One wobble and the rest are at him."

"Like people, don't you think, Ralph? Just like people."

"Take your angelfish, though. That's a separate case. Angelfish mate for life. And when one angelfish goes out of the tank or dies, the other fish will pine for it. One dies and then the other dies, pop-goes-the-weasel. They got the radar, the sick-fish radar. But they stick together for life."

"I'd be the angelfish. Which would you be?"

"Me?" Ralph asks. "You see the donkey, that last donkey making its way down the trail? That's me. I'm an ass. I'm in the scenery. I am the last one to figure it all out."

"I should be the ass, Ralph," I say.

"Zack, you are the whole fucking tank."

■ ■ ■

Patrice is in the downstairs bathroom washing her face. The squeak of faucets and the rush of running water carry through the wall, making the whole house sound like an aquarium, with us the fishes. The tank is in the living room with my blue sofa left over from Shelley and the wall unit that houses the cassette player and CDS. Patrice is screwing around on her husband with Ralph, and Ralph's divorce hasn't come through yet. Once his divorce is finished, Patrice will divorce her husband and then she and Ralph will get together in the house they are building together. That's the plan.

"She's crazy, Zack. We were out hammering on the wall, and it was cold as a motherfuck, when she pulls down my zipper and gives me a blow job. It was so cold, I got on my down parka and gloves. And she just does it."

"You're a grown man, Ralph," I tell him.

"I'll get back to my Word," he says, "but now there is only now."

"I'd like to take the Harley out to the lake some day," I tell him. "I always wanted to go to New Mexico."

"If it wasn't for Shelley, you could be there now."

Patrice comes out of the bathroom. She is twenty-seven, all muscle. Her curly hair is pulled up in a ponytail on the back of her head, and she wears leggings under cutoffs with hiker boots. She comes over, sits in my lap, and gives me a kiss.

"Ralph tell you about the house?" she asks me.

"He says you'll finish by July."

"August at the latest," she says.

"If you ask me, October."

"Nah, Zack. We got to finish before October. The housing market will be bad in October."

"So maybe you two will have to live in it till next June," I say. Patrice gets off my leg and nods to Ralph. She has to go home. She has three kids, none of them by her current husband, but he is rich and takes care of them all. He owns the business that Patrice runs, a construction company. But she loves Ralph. That's the story. That's why he's helping her build the $300,000 house on Smith Mountain Lake. He's got nothing in writing.

Ralph walks her to the door and kisses her good-bye. The rev of her engine sends a ripple through house.

"You got the message from Marianne?" I ask him after Patrice has left the yard.

"Yeah. I came in late last night so I haven't called her back yet."

He dials her from the living room while I am there. While he dials, he watches the zebras pick apart the sick one. "Son of a bitch, he's almost gone," Ralph says. The school drove that one to the bottom, picked at it while it wobbled, picked it into pieces. Its future is obvious. The scavenger fish, the little catfish, will clean up the bottom of the tank.

Ralph doesn't hide anything from me, we are so close. Anything he can say to Marianne, he can say to me. I don't judge him. He doesn't judge me. We have a life.

"When did this happen?" he says to Marianne, pacing around the living room with the cordless phone, pausing in his pacing to see how much of the zebra is left. It is picked apart before his eyes.

"He's been like that since yesterday, and you couldn't take him to the vet? I'll be right over." He turns the phone off, slams it down, and snorts like a horse blowing dust out of its nostrils. Lacing up his boots, Ralph tells me: "Snooker got a fish hook in his lip. She calls me to take him to the vet. Since yesterday, he's been running around with a hook in his mouth. Yesterday! So the poor thing suffers for a night because *I* have to take him to the vet."

"She's trying to get back at you, Ralph."

"For that, the dog suffers."

Marianne is a vindictive woman.

The door slams shut behind him. It's half an hour to his house and then another hour to the vet. That's Marianne. She would call him up to drive over and shut the back door if she could ever get him directly on the phone.

I go into the kitchen and start to wash dishes. Ralph doesn't do them. He is a godly man and a kind man, but his weakness is that he sometimes falls behind on the house stuff. Usually he's so tired from building the house with Patrice, he just comes home and goes to bed. He works full time at B&B making shelves and cabinets for other people, then drives to the lake and works on her house till midnight. It takes him an hour to get home then. He's usually gone before I get up, him leaving extra early to get an Egg McMuffin before he heads down the road.

Before he left Marianne, Ralph owned half a mountain with cattle on it. He had a tractor, a four-bedroom house made of rock with an inlaid rock fireplace he made himself. He put his whole self into that house and then woke up one morning and couldn't live a day more with Marianne. Now he hardly makes his rent here. He gives all his money to Marianne for the kids. He doesn't even have enough money for food. For dinner, he stops at the Jiffy Stop up at the corner, buys himself a quart of "Death by Chocolate" ice cream, and eats the whole thing before he goes to bed. The human body actually needs very little to sustain. Ralph has lost thirty pounds since he began the house.

■ ■ ■

Because I am retired, I don't always know what day it is. The days just roll one into another, and I have difficulty keeping track of time. Because Ralph always leaves early, even on the weekends to work on the house, I can't tell the day by him. Today could be any day. So when the doorbell rings, it could be anyone. People are in and out of here all the time anyhow.

When I answer the front door, I see there are two ladies from the church come to visit me. I have been sickly lately, and, as I said, can't even climb the stairs.

"We haven't seen you in a while, Zack," Mrs. Peachum says. She is about sixty and carries a jar with homemade chicken soup. Her visiting dress has yellow flowers on it, and she wears hose to bring by soup.

"Come in."

I open the door for her. I am still wobbly, so even though I open the door for her, it helps me to keep my balance.

Mrs. Morgan, the preacher's daughter-in-law, is with her. She kisses me on the cheek, saying, "God bless."

"Would you like a cup of tea?" I ask her.

They both would love a cup, so I take the jar with chicken soup into the kitchen and turn on the kettle. But before I make the tea, I slip through the laundry room and climb up the stairs very carefully. In the old days, I could clear three steps in a bound, but now I'm lucky that I don't fall in a pile at the bottom. And now, with church folks in the house, I have something important I have to do.

I make my way to the white bedroom. I shut the door and lock it.

That bedroom was nothing when Shelley was here. It was a junked-up, rotted-wood place with old timbers. I relaid the floor, plastered the walls, put a piece of white carpet in it. My weight machine and free weights leave marks on the white carpet. Because it's the only room in the house with windows on three sides, the sun comes in there the brightest. Ralph built some bookshelves into the wall and in the closet where we store the paint. It's all sunshine and metal up there. Soon Ralph and I will tape up the windows with foil.

I shut the door to this room real tight because Ralph is growing pot plants there. I don't want people from the church to stumble in that room by accident.

I got an honorable testimony.

"We met in church," I argued to convince Shelley. It was only three days since we had met, but I felt the need for the road diminish to a faint hum. I was so in love with her. From the minute I met her, it was love. It was real. That love made me accept everything about her, no questions asked.

"Zack, I'm no good for you."

Shelley watched the sun go down on the beach. She sat on a striped terry-cloth towel and rested back on her elbows. One edge of the towel was folded up over her waist and thighs; her body showed that she was eight years older than me. Her brown hair blew in the wind, and the sun made a flash in the black lens of her sunglasses.

"What is it?" I asked. The sand was piled on my legs and ankles but my feet stuck out of the mound like the Hang-Ten stickers on my hearse. The sun cooked the sand, steaming me inside it.

"I'm out of work now. I can drive truck again."

"You're a good man," she said.

"I saw something in church that I never saw before. That lady talking. What was that about? It wasn't Hebrew."

"Tongues. She speaks in tongues. It's a gift from the Holy Spirit."

"Seemed like nothing to me. A lot of words coming out of her mouth with no order to them. Did they mean anything?"

"The person who speaks them knows what they mean. It's a private language."

"No one interpreted to me."

"God knows what they mean."

"I don't mind about the kid. She seems like a good girl."

"She is."

"So what if you've been married before. It's no big deal."

"You're still a young man. Handsome. You should be running around with single girls."

"I'm getting a settlement soon. From an accident. Twenty-five, maybe thirty thousand dollars. I want to marry you. Forever. Till death do us part. I want to spend the rest of my life with you."

"You don't know what you're talking about."

She pulled up the towel and wrapped it around her hips, started walking toward the waves. They were lapping around her feet by the time I caught up with her.

"You done speaking in tongues to me?"

"So what do you think about New Mexico?" I asked her. "We could take all our stuff and start a new life. I always wanted to see the desert."

"It's the Jew in you," she said. "New Mexico — how about Mexico?"

"I never felt this way about any woman in my life."

"You left your first wife. You'll leave me too when I get old. Just take you a honey jar and a grasshopper if you want the desert effect."

"I prayed to God that I would find you."

"Sure, sure you did, baby."

But she took my hand and we walked down the beach. She came midway up to my chest. I was so attracted to her — it was like magnetism.

"Shelley's not my natural born name," she said in time with

the swinging of our arms. "I was born Rachel. But I didn't want a Jewish name after I converted."

▪ ▪ ▪

Ralph says her funeral was a disgrace. Her mother took her body back to New Jersey. She was buried in a Jewish plot. There was a rabbi there. Six Puerto Ricans, union grave diggers in yellow hard hats, carried her casket to the grave. Ralph stood next to me. We both knew. If either of us said anything about her being a Christian they would have stopped the service. They would have pulled her casket out of the ground. She had come to Christ. But her death was a total disgrace of all that. They buried her as a Jew. We just wanted the service to be over.

▪ ▪ ▪

"What is it, you want me to change my name? Pick one. I'll change it to that. Ronald McDonald? Roy Rogers? Pick one."

"Annie Oakley. Ginger Rogers. Mary Alice."

"Call me Alice. If that's what it takes to make you marry me, I'll change my name. You want a woman's name, you got it."

"I don't want no man telling me how to raise my daughter."

"She's yours. I'll be as much a father to her as I can. I know she's your precious child."

"When do you want to get married?"

"Sunday. This Sunday."

"I won't be able to get a blood test in time. But I have a friend who'll marry us legal without one."

"I'll get the test. You write the vows."

I was so anxious to marry her, I would have done anything, promised anything.

▪ ▪ ▪

Two years, I had waited. Two years my life had been pointless, loveless. It doesn't matter what you have if you don't have someone to love in your life, nothing else matters. Sometimes the wind would come up and blow through my rental, and I'd be eating a burrito from Taco Bell with a beer and watching the late news, and I knew that life had to be more than this. Sometimes I felt like I was sitting around waiting for my destiny to arrive, sometimes I'd even open the door at night to make sure my destiny wouldn't drive by. Every day for me was like a seder at Passover. The Jews open the door for Elijah in case he should come by. But anyone can come in. My every day was like that, me sitting in the dark with a taco, my boots resting on the ottoman, waiting for someone, anyone, Elijah, God, to come in.

I won a belt buckle in a trucking rodeo where I came in third on maneuvering a truck around colored plastic bottles. I got scored for skill and speed. The belt buckle was in the shape of a truck. On nights like this, the buckle would cut up into my stomach over my belt. My undershirt would ride up inside my tucked-in shirt, and my stomach hair would creep out, and I'd find salsa on my belly in the shower.

Me in the dark with salsa on my belly waiting for Elijah, waiting for my destiny.

Me opening the door, watching the wind pass by, hearing the wind whoosh by, watching bright lights carve out the night, calling out, "Come in. Come in."

That's what I was, a man hungry for meeting God at the crossroads.

It turned out that I met this woman.

■ ■ ■

When we got back to the house, Gabrielle was sitting at the kitchen table doing her homework. She had short hair then, cut in a square around her face. She had sweet blue eyes and a few freckles on pink skin.

Shelley put her arm around Gabrielle's shoulders. "Baby, I got a surprise for you."

Gabrielle put down her pencil, looking at me while Shelley continued.

"Zack and I are getting married."

The child turned white in the face; her eyes opened wide. She looked straight at me with a look that could fry fish. Her fist clenched around that pencil and even across the room I could hear her heart beat in four-wheel drive.

"I already have a father," she said.

"Your father and I are divorced," Shelley said.

"What about my father?" Gabrielle said again.

"Go to your room," Shelley said. "I am getting married."

"Mom," she protested.

Shelley grabbed Gabrielle by the shoulder, hauled her out of the chair, and pointed her to the stairwell. "Come back when you can behave yourself."

Gabrielle ran out of the room, crying.

"You didn't have to break it to her so hard," I said.

"Am I her mother or what?"

"All right. All right."

"Her father is a son of a bitch."

"Where is he?" I asked, suddenly wondering if the father would sue for custody. "I can adopt her."

"Never mind. He lives in Miami. He's a drug addict. Shoots up. Picked up the habit in Vietnam."

"Don't worry, baby," I said. "He can't hurt you. I'm here now."

I held her in my arms and brushed the back of her head. At first I thought she was shaking so much from crying, crying for all the pain he must given her, given Gabrielle, but Shelley was shaking with rage, her face white and strained.

"I think you better sleep in the truck tonight."

Shelley went out to the garage to check on the laundry while I used the downstairs bathroom.

In only a couple of days, I had begun to feel at home. The sky-blue sofa in the living room had been my bed for two nights already; my razor lay on top of the toilet. When Shelley was at work — she was a heart nurse at the hospital — I lay on the sofa watching television, waiting for her to come home.

When I came out of the bathroom, I saw Gabrielle with her head bent over her homework, collecting papers to take back with her to her room. When she saw me, she said, "I have a father. And he has — "

Before she could finish, Shelley came into the kitchen with a load of laundry in her arms and said, "Go to your room, Gabrielle. Right this minute. Don't be talking to Zack about private family business."

A flash of defiance streaked across the girl's face. There was a battle going on here, and I was right in the middle of it. This was a time for taking sides, and I wasn't marrying the daughter.

"Poor kid," I said to Shelley. "Does she know about her father?"

"Look, Zack," she said, folding clothes on the kitchen table. "You're giving me double messages. First you say you won't interfere with raising my daughter. Then you interfere. Do you want to get married or not?"

"Baby, you're the boss."

"Go on, then, Zack. Go sleep in the truck tonight. Leave Gabrielle alone. She needs time."

We got married on the beach at Jensen Beach on April 17, 1988, at ten o'clock in the evening with a few witnesses present. We had gone to the courthouse the day before and filled out all the forms, Shelley listing her name as "Shelley Sondheim Moffat." In the place for number of previous marriages, she wrote "one."

I moved into her house, which was a ranch house with a swimming pool. The house belonged to her Uncle Evan, but it was basically hers to live in. She had a brand new car, that Camry. I had my truck and the Harley. The back settlement was pending, but I was looking for work in the day, going around to gas stations to see if I could find something. I read the paper every day.

The more I got to know my new wife, the clearer it became to me that she was a remarkable, intelligent woman. She had books everywhere, not just nursing books but literature books. Her favorites were miniature books of the classics with leather covers on them, a gift from her uncle whom she loved more than her parents. She liked to read the literature books and other books too. She painted as a hobby and had an easel set up in the garage. There was a painting half done on it already: a clown face, one of those sad, white-faced clowns, whose red mouth curved upward on his face. But even though his painted mouth smiled, his actual mouth, the one inside the painted lips, was turned down. He had a red ball nose, but the eyes were so sad. Shelley had started to paint a tear in the corner of his eye. The picture was so good I thought it was a paint-by-number, but it wasn't.

Inside, she had curtains on all the windows. Not plain down-hanging curtains or sheets, but fancy curtains with sashes and knots and ribbons strung from them. She had a marble topped coffee table with a lamp that had a man on it. The man lay stretched on his side with his legs out. He wore funny shorts and a lumpy hat, and he lay like he was stretched out in nature, leaning up against the base of a tree, which turned into the base of the lamp.

Once I asked her, "Who is this motherfuck?"

She said, "Don't talk like a truck driver. This is Goethe."

"Who is Gerter?" I asked.

She said, "You found any work yet?"

One day, after I mowed the front lawn with a hand-push

mower, I felt pretty tired. So I got a beer from the fridge and took a swim in the pool in my shorts. After a couple of strokes, I climbed into a lawn chair, lay my towel over my head and took a snooze. When Gabrielle came home from school, she came out to the back, pulled up a lawn chair next to me and started talking. That beer made all sounds fuzzy round the edges. Gabrielle seemed to be talking about her father from a place in outer space. I nodded every now and then to let her know I was following her in a random pattern, but the truth is, I didn't know what the hell she was saying except that she was agitated. That agitation made me fade out on her more.

When Shelley came home, I heard her call through the kitchen window. "Gabrielle, come in the house this minute."

I heard them arguing through the window, Shelley asking what Gabrielle was doing with me half naked around the pool, what we were talking about, the whole business.

Then Shelley came out to the pool and started ragging my ass about my getting work.

"Baby, baby," I said to her, "I am *trying* to find work."

"Trying? With your ass in the lawn chair?"

"Shelley, I mowed the lawn. Go outside to the front yard and look at your lawn. The mower's still out front, leaning against the wall."

"Summer is coming. I don't want you and Gabrielle hanging around the pool all summer. And you drinking beer." She had a voice like a chain saw when she got worked up. She kept cutting away at me, asking *did you hear from the insurance company yet, why don't you get on it, who do you think you are, a lazy bum who didn't have to work, a useless good for nothing, she had to get up every morning to go to work, and for what?*

"Look," I said. "What's this about Gabrielle's father? She was talking like he was still around."

"He's as good as dead."

The next day, Shelley quit her job.

For no reason I gave her, she didn't want me to be alone in the house with her daughter.

I told her, "Shelley, we need the money."

She told me: "I don't want you alone in the house with Gabrielle."

We were married for a month before I realized that Shelley was all over my ass. I said to myself, "What am I doing with my life? I don't know this woman." We fought like cats and dogs. I decided to leave her. I got in my pickup truck, proceeded to pull out, and made my mind up that I was leaving. I almost got out of the driveway. But you know, as you back out, you look in front of you also. When I looked in front of me, I saw that ten-year-old daughter looking at me through the screen door. I didn't have the heart to break that kid's heart because she really wanted a father. For the sake of that kid, I came back.

I left the house for five minutes.

And then I came back.

"I thought you were going to the 7-11," Shelley said. "Did you bring me my cigarettes?"

"I want to have a family outing," I said. "Let's go to A&W Root Beer and get floats."

"You hear that Gabrielle," Shelley said, "Zack's taking us out for a root beer float."

She said, "How did he know that was my favorite?"

We piled into my truck with Gabrielle squeezed up in between me and Shelley. One minute I was ready to leave and the next we were on a family outing. It felt family-like to me, my wife and my daughter and me going for a float. I wished there had been somebody around I could give a dollar to and say, "Take this picture."

"Is Jennings home?" I asked Shelley as she rolled down the window. Jennings was an old retired veteran who lived in the house next door, and he kept a Polaroid camera around because he kept care of his grandkids during holidays.

"No," she said. "Why?"

"I would pay Jennings money to take our picture. 'The Family Outing.'" I laughed and honked the horn for fun.

Shelley carried a big carpetbag, loaded to the top with cigarettes. As we drove down the road, she kept saying, "I'm going to quit. I need to quit. And I will quit."

That was a family thing too, with people trying to improve, to make themselves better. They say over and over the one thing that will improve their lives but never do it. That really made me feel like I was in a family then because the other family members listen, and they love the improver anyhow, so it has a kind of charm to it.

Gabrielle was squeezed in between us. She was at the age where her bangs were too long and stuck in her eyes, so she kept brushing her bangs and shaking her head. But she was starting to develop a flair in the way she shook off her bangs, so it had a dramatic edge to it. At the A&W Root Beer, the waitress came out to the car with three floats on a tray that she hooked over the edge of the window. All three floats were the same but Gabrielle reached over and pointed to the one in the middle, saying she wanted that one. "Your mother first," I told her, and passed her a float to give to Shelley. She said all right and flipped her hair. Both Gabrielle and her mother liked to drink the root beer half way down before they ate the scoop of vanilla ice cream, but I always started at the ice cream first because I liked to lick it off my mustache. After Gabrielle made sucking noises in the straw, she belched, and Shelley told her to stop.

"Do you believe this, Zack? This morning she asked when she could start wearing lipstick. And now she belches."

"She's too young to wear lipstick."

I just said it innocently, not meaning to interfere in any way with her mother-daughter relationship. Gabrielle sucked air through the straw on purpose. Shelley told me to call the waitress, and we would drink the rest of our floats at home because her daughter didn't know when to keep quiet.

"You think I'm too fat, Zack?" Shelley asked me as we pulled out, nothing left of her float but a line of froth around the edge of her cup.

"You're perfect," I told her. After all, she was a forty-year-old woman. She tipped the scales at about a hundred and fifty, but it was all woman. I liked a full-bodied woman. She unbuttoned her slacks as we drove home.

When we came around the corner, stopping at the stop sign, I saw two guys standing on the corner talking.

"Is it the Fourth of July a'ready?" I asked.

"Why?" Shelley asked.

"What are folks doing out on a hot day like this, jawing in their yard?"

"It's not folks," said Shelley. "It's just two men. What's the matter, Zack, you can't count?"

"I was exaggerating. For fun. Don't you get it?"

"It's just two guys."

It was strange to see them out on their yards, already low cut, without mowers or washing a car. Just two guys, one thin and yellow talking to another with an army cap on. A little reminder of Vietnam, which I never went to. My number never came up, but if it had, I think I would have left the country and gone to Canada. Not that I've ever been a coward. But I wasn't that involved in national happenings. It might have been good for me, I think, to have joined the marines. But they would never take me voluntarily. I never finished my high school education. Nor passed my G.E.D.

Gabrielle gulped air. "That's *David*," she said.

"That's not David," Shelley said. "That's a dying David."

"Who's David?" I asked about the guy, standing on the corner. He was really thin, stood like his legs hurt, all the weight shifting back and forth. Like a smoker, he had yellow-colored skin and bags under his eyes.

"Wasn't David your ex-husband's name?" I asked.

"It was," she said, but before I could ask any more, we passed down the road, around the block, home, and Shelley was hopping out of the truck. "Don't move." She shut the door on us. "I'm going to get my camera."

Then she took a picture of me and Gabrielle through the front window. I put my straw in Gabrielle's float, and she and I drank from the same cup through two separate straws. "I sure am glad I got this straw," I said to Gabrielle with my lips around my straw. "I always get ice cream in my mustache."

"Stop talking, Zack. You want to ruin this picture?"

Then Gabrielle took my picture with Shelley, and I put my arm around her. That picture of us together as a happy family made me forget the question I had put to her about David. Who he was, why he was important.

That's how happiness works. When you get a little bit of it, you want to hang on with all your heart. It's like driving straight. You don't look into the bushes, under the dark edges of things. You just stay between the lines and look straight ahead.

Shelley was quit of her nursing job for two weeks, and we were still waiting for the insurance settlement for my back injury. Our money was running low. The lower it ran, the more we wanted that check to get us out of Florida. Even though we were broke, we didn't do anything about it. There are some things in my life I am not proud of, and I'm not proud of us sitting around like lazy bums. Sometimes we lay in the bed until noon. Sometimes we'd get up for a skinny-dip and go back to bed, drinking wine the whole time. Two lazy bums, sitting around and waiting for the money to come through.

"You ever think about Frieda?" she asked me.

"No." This was true. Or if I did think about her, I thought about her in the past tense.

"I think of David sometimes. I really loved David. But he ruined my life."

"Yeah, right," I said.

I went out to sit by the pool, wondering what she meant by that. Some of my free weights were left out there, so I sat in a lawn chair and curled little two-pound weights with my wrist, counting up, "One, two, three, four, five . . ."

One. Here she was, with a brand-new car, a three-bedroom house, a new husband. *Two.* We were planning to make a new life. *Three.* We were waiting on a settlement check, so money was on the way. *Four.* Everything in her life was ahead of her. With so much ahead of her, I didn't understand why she kept looking back.

Shelley acted like there was a movie she had seen but I hadn't. She kept referring to parts or scenes from it. Even when she didn't directly refer, she'd indirectly refer to it. If she saw a man and a woman standing on a street having a quarrel, she'd say, "The son of a bitch. That's men."

I had my own movie going too, sure. If I saw a man and woman having a quarrel in the street, I'd think that the man was defending himself against the woman because she was ready to stick it to him with a knife. Shelley would see the opposite, that the woman was sticking it to the man because he already hit her. To her, the woman was protecting herself. To me, it was the man acting in self-defense. But I had this view because of my life with my mother, and so even though I had this movie, I understood where I was sitting and how things looked to me from this seat. But Shelley thought there was only one movie or one script, and it didn't matter what I did or did not do, she connected a part of me to her movie. Men to her were sons-a-bitches and useless. But she still said she loved me.

"Zack," Shelley called me through the screened-in bedroom window. I had been working out by the pool for twenty minutes. "Zack, come in here."

She was lying spread-eagled on the top of the bed, totally naked. Her vibrator was lying next to her. Her eyes were hungry, with a glazed look like when a deer dies or the gaze of a hawk when it sights a mouse. She put her finger in her pussy and rubbed there, calling me. I pulled down my shorts and she wrapped her arms around my neck, biting my ear, saying, "I feel so lonely, baby. Baby, baby, please fuck me up the ass."

I had never done it before, but I rolled her over. I reached around and squeezed her breasts, they filled both my hands, and she liked it when I squeezed them so hard, she gasped in pain. Her asshole was so tight. I don't know how anybody could stand being fucked up the ass, but it felt so good, and she made my cock so hard, I couldn't hear anything, feel anything but the four-wheel drive drumming through my head coming out my cock. She was gasping, all sweaty. Then she rolled over and said, "Lick my pussy." Which I did, doing it the way she liked it. Then she asked me to give her the vibrator, which I did. And then she wanted to shove it up my ass, her rolling me over and licking my ass, then raising the vibrator and trying to stick it up my asshole. But I seized up and couldn't take it, so I rolled over on my back, panting, laying there next to her, and she lay next to me, stuck a tittie in my mouth. When I woke up a few hours later, her tit was still in my mouth.

We did not make love until we had gotten married, but after that we did everything. Shelley took me to places I had never been. At night, in the bed, she talked to me, talked dirty, which made me excited. She'd say, "Hurt me, Zack," or "I'm evil. Punish my pussy." She made me dress up in her underwear. Then she would put on my clothes, my black pants, a white shirt, and a tie. She shoved her hair under one of my hats. Then we would lie in front of the mirror, her sitting in front of me so my cock came up between her legs. She would run it through her underwear, so it looked like she had an erection. "That's my cock," she said, looking at herself in the mirror, opening the buttons in my shirt till her tits hung out, and she squeezed her own nipples with long fingernails, me saying, "It's your cock, baby. You got a beautiful cock. Look at how hard it is."

At first she'd tell me, "Zack, we're married. We're consenting adults. Anything we do is all right because we are married." I believed her, though I had never done it like that with Frieda. Frieda never liked to have sex on the top. But Shelley was on top, in front, behind, every way you could turn, she did. Frieda never liked to have sex when she was on her period. With Shelley, it was different. As soon as she got a little blood in her panties, she'd get excited. Sometimes she would point to the blood on the sheet and say, "You fucked me till I bled, baby." Then she'd slap me. Maybe sometimes she would cry or stare at her blood in the bed, saying, "That's my blood. My blood is on you."

I am not a smart man or an educated man. How could I know she was leading up to something? I couldn't know until I knew, and then it was too late. But at the time, it seemed like play-acting or sex play and the line between normal relations and those extra-charged sex-playing actions faded away. Later, when I thought about it, she could have been dying beneath me and screaming from pain, but since our sex was so kinked up then, I would have thought it was a new game or a new scenario and never thought twice about it. My experience had never prepared me for anyone like Shelley. Frieda liked a straight fuck, but Shelley took me on the wild side. Once you done it all the ways you could never think of, you can't go back to straight sex. Shelley asked me to do things to her that she must have gotten out of a book because no one would tell about it.

But came Sunday morning, we were dressed in nice clothes and saying, "Praise the Lord." Her house had white carpets and white linoleum. She hung ferns in the window. The grass was neat. The pool was clear.

You could not tell by the outside what was happening on the inside.

 On a Sunday morning we went to church, a respectable family of two Jews for Jesus. Gabrielle didn't like to come with us, but sometimes Shelley made her. Sateen got some new speakers in, he told me after church. Even though he knew I was broke, he thought I'd still be interested, plus we liked to look at the catalog for Harley parts.

I told Shelley I was going to take out the bike. She said I should be home by five for supper. I rode out in my leathers, and

Sateen and I sat behind the counter on two old orange crates, flipping through the catalog.

"How's married life?" he asked me.

"Fine," I told him. "But times are tough since my wife quit her job."

"What'd she quit for?" he asked.

"Don't know. She just quit."

"Too bad," he said. "She was a damn fine nurse. She worked on Cheryl Roger's mama when she had the bypass."

"I believe it. She's good at everything she does."

"But you know, Zack," he added. "I'm just telling you this because we are friends in the Lord: your wife has a high temper."

"That she does. It's the change. Women get high strung when they go through it."

"Maybe," he said, "but some folks think she is as crazy as a loon."

"What's a loon?" I asked.

"Let me show you these speakers," he said.

I was five minutes late coming in the door. Shelley had the table set and dinner on the table, pork chops and mashed potatoes. "You son of a bitch," she said. "I told you to be home at five. To think I did all this work for nothing. Going out on a Sunday like a Hell's Angel. Are you fucking some little waitress on the side?"

I don't know where she had gotten this idea because I was strictly faithful. I was the kind of biker who would help a lady change a tire.

She pushed all the dishes off the table. She pulled the tablecloth off the table and threw it in the sink. She threw the little dinner buns at me, which, thank the Lord, were soft. All the while she cursed me. "You are no good. Good for nothing, not even for fucking. I got a dildo works better than you, you limp-dicked, two-timing prick."

I walked outside to the backyard by the pool. I sat by the water and watched the sun glisten in the blue water. We had talked enough about starting a new life, and I was ready for it. But that check had not come. When it came, it would make a difference in our lives, a real difference. Maybe it was the place that made her crazy, this too-little town where people remembered her first husband. He must have hurt her, I think, because a woman doesn't learn the things she knew from nature. She got the poison from the place, from the past, from that man. She was spreading that poison on to me.

I tried to recall my special vision. "Look up," said the Lord. *Faith, prayer.* My faith told me I had consecrated my life to her in love. I had faith that Shelley would come to feel comfortable in love, that the hard edges of her heart would melt. I prayed that she would change, that the check would come, that we could start a new life. We would get in the truck, drive north, and put the past behind us. Even though David was out of her life, so she said, living now in Miami, so she said, he was still around, still in her life, still present in her mind.

A new beginning. The Lord gives us that when we take Him into our lives. That's the meaning of baptism, to be baptized in the Lord, to be cleansed. To begin again.

But I was confused about my life. God had given me a sign for my soul mate, my *b'sherta:* a Leviticus Jew converted to Christianity. I had been looking for a sign. I had done everything in order. I found her, recognized her, married her. Even though I had been promiscuous as a teenager, I had waited till we were married to make love to her. I had followed all the steps, yet something seemed out of whack. The overall mood of my marriage did not feel like that of a Christian marriage.

I wanted to feel closer to my God, that God of the Jews and of the Christians alike. My eyes searched the sky for a thunder cloud. I wanted God, my Father, to speak to me. It was a clear day. All I could see was the tops of trees with hanging moss and the telephone poles that faded into the horizon. I wanted a repeat of my vision. As I sat by the pool, my eyes searched the sky. They found only a broad expanse of clear blue.

No lightning. No thunder. No signs.

 I liked the feel of her clothes, and my hands were on a silk dress, turquoise with green-and-yellow swirls, with pleats down the front. The colors brought out Shelley's eyes. But now her beautiful new silk dress was draped on the cotton bedspread of a two-bit motel. Fleabag digs are all right for a trucker, and some nights when I didn't have a dime to my name I slept in drainage pipes. But they never wash the bedspreads in these hotels, and this dress was one of the first things she bought after my settlement check came in. It was a sixty-dollar dress and the first time she had worn it was for her job interview in Charlotte, North Carolina.

How did we come to be camped out in fleabag digs in North Carolina?

We were starting our new life.

Back in Florida, as soon as Shelley got the check in her hands, she went on a shopping spree. She even bought shoes to match the dress and earrings to match everything. Then we went to the makeup section at a store in the mall. Shelley had her face made up while I hung around the counter, holding her bag.

"You need more moisturizer," the cosmetologist said. She looked twenty in a pink-striped smock, like a young, blond candy cane.

"Can you guess my age?" Shelley asked.

The candy cane girl said, "Thirty-seven."

"Then maybe I don't need moisturizer," Shelley said.

"Those girlish looks."

She continued to powder up Shelley's cheeks, outlined her lips with a pencil. "Most husbands don't like to wait around on their wives," she said to both of us. "If you want to set your purchases down, I can put them behind the counter."

"I don't mind holding 'em," I said.

"Zack, hand me a stick of gum, will you."

She was still trying to quit smoking.

At the end of the procedure, Shelley looked at herself in the mirror while the cosmetologist showed her all the little pots of color she had put on her face and eyes. Shelley eventually handed me another bag, it even had moisturizer in it, to carry as we went through the mall.

"You think she was attractive, Zack?" Shelley put on her sunglasses, wide lenses, black frames that wrapped around her face.

"She was all right. She looked like Gabrielle."

"I wish I could have met you sooner. I'd like to look young for you."

"You're perfect, Shelley."

"You always say that. I saw you looking at her."

"I wasn't looking at her."

"Don't lie to me. I saw you."

"She mighta been in my line of sight. That's all."

"First you said you weren't looking and then you said you were. You're giving me double messages."

"Shelley, you're my wife. I think you're beautiful. I love you."

"You like older women. I forgot. Until they get too old."

Shelley walked down the mall ahead of me and wouldn't say another word until we got home, and then she tried on that turquoise dress and all the things that went with it.

Most women get excited doing a striptease, but she got hot putting on all those clothes in front of me, first the slip and the hose, the dress, the earrings. After she was decked out and admired herself in the mirror on all sides, she pulled up the hem of her dress.

"Zack, I forgot something. I forgot to put on my underwear."

"Let me kiss it, baby," I said pushing her down on the waterbed.

■ ■ ■

We dropped a wad at the mall where Shelley went all out on that dress. That settlement for my back injury burned a hole in both our pockets. Following our hopes and dreams, Shelley and I got in my truck, driving north, not west, to make our new life. We left Gabrielle with a sitter for the week or so we'd be gone. Shelley thought New York state would be good because it had lots of open country. We wanted a place far from the city but near enough for us to work. We started driving. The first place we stopped was Asheville, North Carolina, but that place was a tourist trap, and we couldn't see any way to make a decent living. We went on. In Charlotte, Shelley dressed in the turquoise dress to start looking for jobs.

I really wanted to go to New Mexico. I lay in the bed in the hotel in Charlotte with the map in front of me all morning, studying the routes and counting miles. I counted miles all through "Good Morning, America." If you could have seen me, you would have known I was my father's son, making equations between cities. It was about seven hundred miles to New York City, but if we went west we could maybe reach Arkansas. It took about the same amount of miles to reach Canada as it took to reach St. Louis.

When Shelley came back to the hotel, I told her, "This place is too overpopulated."

"I like it, Zack."

"I couldn't live here."

She threw off her dress on the spread.

"We both have to like the place. We agreed," I said.

"Yeah, right."

She went into the bathroom, locked the door, and ran bath water. I could hear it from the bedroom while I turned down the television and hung up her dress in the closet. I held that dress in my hands for a minute, silk so soft it felt like cool running water slipping through my hands. It had her smell on it, a smell with roses in it.

I was so in love with my wife.

Somewhere down the road, a siren screeched like there was a fire. It seemed to go on and on. The map lay open on the unmade bed. We would have to go north to get to 40 West. But Shelley had been in the bath a while, and I was getting lonely. Sirens made me edgy. I wondered why she would take a bath so early in the day since she had taken one before she left. The cops were always on my ass when I was a boy growing up. I got chased by the cops on foot and in the car. Shelley was in there too long to be taking a bath.

I knocked on the door. "You hear those sirens, Shelley?"

She didn't say anything. I knocked again. "Shelley, you hear the sirens? Are you all right?"

Still no answer. I hit on the door.

She yelled, "Leave me alone."

I took a bobby pin from the dresser and picked the lock. Shelley was sitting in the bathtub in her slip. Her legs were bent in the bath, and she leaned back, with the water about six inches up her leg. She had taken my razor and tried to cut through one of her wrists. Blood was everywhere, in the tub, on the bath mat. My razor rested on the side of the tub.

"My God," I said. I grabbed a hand towel off the rack and wrapped it around her wrist to stop the bleeding. Her face was red and puffy from sobbing.

I put my arms under her armpits, dragged her out of the tub, her feet making a slippery sound as they scraped the bottom. I grabbed a bath towel and wrapped it around her body so she wouldn't get cold in the air-conditioning and carried her to the bed.

When I picked up the phone, she asked, "What are you doing?"

"I am calling 911," I said.

"No, please. Please. Don't do it. DON'T do it. I'm all right. Just get me some ice."

I ran outside to the ice machine and got a bucketful of ice. She took her good hand and rolled up the ice in the towel and covered the wound in her wrist. She was gulping air as she did it, like she was hysterical.

"It's all right. It's all right," she said between the gulps.

Because she was a surgical nurse, I believed her. She knew what she was doing. Even though she was hysterical, she still stopped the bleeding in her wrist. I didn't think of it at the time, but I did later: a nurse would have known how to cut her own wrist to do serious damage. But she hadn't cut through any tendons or ligaments. She had made a bloody cut but not a life-threatening one. I wasn't thinking at the time. At the time I was thinking my wife was so distraught she would take her own life.

"Talk to me, Shelley," I begged her. "What's wrong, baby? Why are you so unhappy?"

"There's something I haven't told you, Zack," she said.

"Tell me. Tell me. You can tell me anything. I love you. I married you." I was practically hysterical myself.

"It's about my other marriage."

"Fine. Fine." I wrapped my arms around her and held her close to my chest. There was no blood coming off her arm anymore, although the hand towel had a big red stain.

"I was pregnant before. After Gabrielle."

"What happened?"

"It was twins. I carried them seven months."

"Shh. Shh. What happened? What happened to the twins?"

"I met this guy in a bar. He was going to give me a ride home on his motorcycle. So I said OK. But something happened. The twins got turned around inside me. From the bike. I went to the doctor, I was feeling so sick. He said the twins were dead. Dead inside me. And so I had an operation. He took them out. But they weren't dead. They died after he took them out."

I ran my hand down the back of her hair. She was a middle-aged woman quivering like a rabbit in my hand, shaking all through her. I could feel her heart tremble.

"It's all right. All right, baby."

"I lost the twins," she said and burst out crying again. "Sometimes I think of them. I miss them so much. They were boys. Both boys. They turned around."

We stayed an extra night at the hotel. I wrung out her slip and underwear, washed the blood stains out of them, and hung them over the shower bar to dry. I brought in hamburgers from McDonald's, and we watched a movie. Shelley lay tucked up close under my arm, falling in and out of sleep. When I felt her head, it was hot. When she woke up, she asked me to get her some aspirin, which I did. We fell asleep with the TV on, but in the middle of night she broke into a sweat. She was wet and clammy to the touch. I turned off the air-conditioning and covered her with a sheet; even the sheet got wet from her sweating. Sweating, she was freezing, shaking from chills.

"Just get me some more aspirin," she said. When I did, she

left the bed to run for the bathroom. She had a bad case of diarrhea as well. I finally had to roll to the far side of the bed where it was dry before I could close my eyes to get some sleep.

I don't answer my phone anymore. Either I let the answering machine pick it up or Ralph gets it. Marianne calls here four and five times a day asking for Ralph. If I answer it, she will ask me *where is he? is he with that woman from work? why doesn't he call me right back? you know the truth, don't you, Zack, and you are covering up for Ralph, he won't ever get away from me, we are married for life, Zack, he's still my husband, the divorce isn't final yet, I want to talk to my husband, where is he?*

Everything with her is urgent. The wind blew the screen door off her back door once at midnight, and she called Ralph to tell him there was an emergency. He went then to fix the door, and it was after midnight. "She's never done anything for herself," he told me. She counted on him three hundred percent, and until the divorce is finalized, she keeps trying to get him back.

I don't like to answer it. My phone is hooked up to a screening device that shows the number ringing my house. One time the phone rang, and the readout said: "Out of Area." It was Gabrielle.

"I don't know if you remember me," she left the message. "I was your stepdaughter. I, um, I just wanted to call and tell you that my brother had a baby."

I don't like to get stressed out by taking calls. What did she expect? Shelley's creditors called me years after she was gone. Some call me even now and ask for her. But as I don't answer, I don't call them back. Sooner or later, they will figure out that there is no one here by that name.

When Ralph comes home, he and I sit in front of the Grand Canyon, me drinking tea, him with a quart of ice cream on his lap. I wonder why his legs don't get cold from it. We watch the fish like we used to watch the Harley.

I say to him, "Ralph, some people from the church came by the other day. I want you to get rid of the plants."

"Sure, buddy," he says. "They're your plants. I got them for you."

"There are church people here all the time. What if my pastor comes over and — "

"We'll do it right now."

He takes one big bite out of the chocolate, grabs a big plastic garbage bag, and we go upstairs to the white room. Between the two of us, we sweep all the pot plants into the garbage bag. Seventeen pot plants four inches high. Right into the trash.

That's what I love about Ralph. All I have to do is ask and he is there for me. We cleared those plants out faster than we thought we could do it. In fact, we cleaned them out so fast, the house-cleaning urge still bothered us though it was midnight.

"The trash bag still has room in it," he says. "Why don't we clear out some other junk."

"Great."

We go downstairs to his room, which used to be the Harley room until Shelley put her books in it. Now it is Ralph's room, but the shelves are made into the wall and they cover one wall. Ralph built himself a bed in that room. He used to go out to the woods and drag home huge tree branches. He made a four-poster bed out of raw wood with the knots still in it. He made the base from planks, into which he carved a design. He had a Native American thing, so it looks like an Indian bed. I don't know what he'll do if he ever moves. He'd have to take the whole thing apart to move it.

He was studying the bookshelves where Shelley's old books remain. Some are nursing books. Some are her favorites, those leather classic books in miniature.

"You need to get rid of these, Zack," he says. He lifts up one heavy book, a psychology book.

"I need that book, Ralph," I tell him.

"Which book is it?"

He reads the title on the spine, then says, "Oh yeah."

It was proof.

Ralph and I came to the same conclusion together the day we went through her things. In one of her psychology nursing books, Shelley had underlined all the remarks about paranoid schizophrenia. In the front, she had written notes:

Symptoms

1) Disordered thinking

   bizarre ideas

   ability to concentrate and to organize thoughts

   *Loose association

   lack of goal direction

■ ■ ■

That's what made us think that she thought she was schizophrenic, that she was trying to puzzle out her own nature.

Ralph's fingers close around one little book, Shakespeare's sonnets. He cracks the spine and opens it, reads a few lines. He reads it out loud because he loves poetry and reading. He used to help his kids with homework. The music of the words pulls him into the poem. At first, he's really into it; then he stops a second, like he has been tricked, and tosses the book into the trash bag with the pot plants.

"The murderess," he says.

13 Shelley got a nursing job at Roanoke City Hospital in Virginia. I got a job hauling paper with Corrugated Cardboard. The runs were day jobs only, no more long-distance driving for me, but I came home very late. Gabrielle would be in bed when I got home. Usually Shelley would leave some supper for me on the stove, covered with aluminum foil. I would shower and climb into bed with her. Then she would roll over and kiss me good night. The check had come through, and we would be fine. She had told me about the twins that had died. That had been weighing heavily on her heart for a long time. I accepted that. Just as I accepted her with no questions asked. Because I was an honorable man and I married her and I took in her daughter. Besides, our new life was about to begin.

Our new state. Our new house. Our new life.

I had the bike with me, and I used to like to drive along the Parkway. For no reason. Just to take the bike out. (Sometimes Ralph and I laugh about that expression, "take the bike out." It sounds like going on a date with the bike. But it was something special, that Harley. It deserved to be taken out on a date!) The Parkway is a scenic road in Virginia that is so fine that the road department closes it when it snows. If they salted the road, the salt would damage the asphalt. The Parkway runs through rolling hills and the local mountains. In the spring, the leaves are so thick you can't see around the bend. In the winter, you see that there were mountains behind the trees, and you still can't see the bend.

On the Parkway, a bridge passes three hundred feet over the New River. When I went out on the Harley, I rode over it all the time. You could stand on the bridge and look down into brown, chopping water cracking into white froth on rocks. A woman from our church jumped from the bridge when she learned she had cancer. It turned out that the diagnosis was wrong. On my rides, I would stop at the top of the bridge and look down, wondering why that woman did not give life a chance to reveal itself to her. She was in such a hurry to end it, but she didn't have all the facts. It was a long drop.

A month after we had moved in permanently, Shelley got a call from her uncle, the one with the ranch house and pool. When she hung up, she said, "David is dead."

Gabrielle's father.

"What did he die of?" I asked her.

"Cirrhosis of the liver."

Making sandwiches for a picnic she had been planning for the two of us, Shelley started talking like I wasn't there at all. "I loved David. But he ruined my life."

"What are you talking about? How did he ruin your life?"

She didn't say anything. When I started reading the paper, she looked at me with flat, black eyes.

We took the Harley out, riding along the Parkway, crossing over the bridge. Twenty miles south, we stopped at a grassy spot, parked the bike, and looked around for a place to have the picnic. The woods were so thick we couldn't see what was over a hill, so we explored the area up the hill. We found an old graveyard with carved tombstones.

"I want to eat here," Shelley said, walking through the headstones, trailing her hand over the tops of them.

"Did you bring any sunscreen?" I asked her.

She said, "I can never forget. Death always finds me."

"What are you talking about?" I asked her.

She said, "Put the blanket down here, Zack."

She sat on a grassy bank and leaned against a headstone. An

angel was carved in the top, and she read the name and the date out loud.

I thought she was talking about David. The twins. That woman had so much loss in her life. Her life had been full of suffering. She was so young to know so much. I knew I couldn't make up for any of that. But I loved her with all my heart.

When we drove further up the Parkway, we found a place in the grass behind the millstone, and I made love to her in the way she liked the best.

 I got this terrible pain on the head of my penis. When I got up one morning to take a leak, it was covered with sores, open sores, and it hurt like hell for me to pass urine. I didn't know what it was. I had run around on Frieda when we were married, and sometimes I screwed women I didn't know when I was driving truck in Florida, but I hadn't been with anyone for two years before I met Shelley.

I called her from the doctor's office. Dr. Hank Phillips had a private practice five miles into town, so it was close to the hospital where Shelley worked as a cardiac nurse. Dr. Phillips's office was a building with white planks and wide windows that looked like a house, with a steep driveway leading up to the parking lot. I waited in the parking lot for Shelley to come. I waited by walking around my truck. I walked a hundred turns in one direction, and then I walked a hundred turns in the other. I did this for more repeats than I could keep track of until I saw the nose of the Camry edge up the steep hill. It came up slowly, me seeing the car by parts, the line of the roof, the chrome bumper, two lights like eyes, a stretch of windshield with the sun reflecting off it. Shelley pulled over slowly to the side and rolled down the window.

I looked at her through the window like the day I had first seen her parked on the oyster-shell lot of the Baptist church in Florida. That time, I had looked at her and seen a reflection of myself, my heritage, my belief in God. I had never felt so at home in the world as I did on that day. But this time, as I bent in to stare at my reflection in her sunglasses, as she tapped her nails on the dashboard, her carpetbag open on the passenger seat, bottles of aspirin spilling over the top, I saw her as a total stranger. She could have been from Mars for all the feeling I had for her.

"Guess what," I told her, "I got a venereal disease."

"You son of a bitch." She slapped my face through the window. Then she rolled it up, peeled rubber out of the driveway and pulled out with the brake lights fading as she drove down the hill.

She thought I'd given it to her.

No man could have been more faithful to her than me. With her crying spells, with her rage and loss, with her hurricanes of feeling so great the house could not contain them, any other man would have left her. Another man would have walked out long ago. But I never got rid of the taste of failure left from my first marriage. It never went away. I believed that if I loved her enough, if I prayed enough, something would change.

I asked Dr. Phillips how I had gotten it.

"You sexually promiscuous?" he asked me.

"No. I been faithful to my wife, and even before, I didn't sleep with anyone."

"Has your wife had other partners?"

"She's been married before."

"Maybe her former husband infected her. You had to get it from somewhere, Mr. Rosen. You don't just get a venereal disease like it grows up in you from cancer."

Shelley didn't let me sleep in our bed for two weeks. She didn't speak to me, and she wouldn't cook. She didn't clean. When she looked at me, her eyes were filled with contempt. I might have tried to talk it out with her, but she had nothing to say to me except, "I want the Harley out of the house."

The downstairs spare bedroom was the Harley room where I kept my bike when I wasn't riding it. My toolbox was down there, with my tools laid out on a piece of newspaper. My chest of drawers — five white-oak, deep drawers — was filled with sprockets, a hand brake, an exhaust pipe. Above the chest of drawers, pictures of me with my Harley, with my first three cars including the Cadillac Eureka, were nailed to the wall.

I moved the bike outside to the front porch.

The next time I went to take the bike out for a ride, Shelley stood inside behind the screen door. "You taking it out for a ride?"

"Yeah," I said.

"You going to pick up another piece of ass?"

"It's my bike."

"Son of a bitch."

 "Baby," Shelley called me from the bed, "Give Mama some sugar." She had a cold, so her flannel nightgown was buttoned up to her neck. She had her reading glasses on, and her eyes looked like two gray-green marbles behind the lenses. She called to me through the doorway because I was downstairs pulling out rotted planks from the porch.

I was sweaty with huge stains around my T-shirt. I must have stunk worse than George at the Peaches Galore, but I was so happy to be welcomed again into the fold that I fell into her arms. I kissed her like I was Moses in the Promised Land, so grateful that she still loved me, that she still wanted me. We made love through the bedclothes, tearing the sheets off the bed and leaving them in piles on the floor.

One day I was a son of a bitch, the next day she wanted Daddy to give her some sugar. I could live with that when today was the day she wanted loving.

Later, we went downstairs and she made a pot of coffee, pouring it for me as I sat at the kitchen table, kissing my neck.

"I want you to do something for me, baby," she said.

"Yeah?"

"You should see what I see coming through the emergency room. Boys that wreck. Their bodies are cut into pieces. Their skin is shredded like it's been through a machine. Glass cuts through the leathers. But that's not what I want. I am going to make a change on our life-insurance policy. You don't need to worry about it."

"Sure."

I would have agreed to anything to have her back loving on me. She kissed me on the back of the neck, saying, "Baby, I am so, so sorry."

I didn't know what she meant.

I only felt her kisses, and her kisses filled up everything.

Shelley handled all the household paperwork. She did our taxes, she helped me fill out employment forms. While I could read and write, I wasn't very good at it. Sometimes I thought it was a concentration problem, but I spent hours on my bike working with small parts. I could hold a nine thousand–gallon tanker truck in between the yellow lines for six hundred miles. I could take apart a wooden porch and put it back together again.

One time Shelley told me, when she was painting in the garage in Florida, "You had so much potential."

No one ever heard of a Jewish truck driver. People think brains come with the nose. My people have been bankers, thinkers, writers, merchants. Every Jew I ever met had gone right to the top, but with me it was the opposite. Sometimes I wondered if I had a gene missing, because my brothers, even my baby brother, Frankie, were making six-digit salaries. The in-between brother, Murray, had worked his way through college while selling airplanes and eventually ended up as CEO for an international airplane dealership. Once I saw him on a news program. The camera showed him in a hotel in Baltimore putting on a benefit dinner for children with cancer. He wore a tuxedo with a white jacket. A flying magazine used him in its advertisement. There was my brother, this time in a black-jacket tuxedo, with a skinny girl in a dress like a slip and pouring him a glass of champagne in front of a red twin-engine Cessna. "What does Murray Rosen drink?" was written under it. When he was chosen for *Cosmopolitan* magazine's Bachelor of the Month, he became a celebrity.

Frankie had a car dealership in Atlanta. He owned two houses, one to live in and one he bought as an investment. He had a nice wife, two kids, and a dog. Me, I was the Woodstock survivor. I dug rock 'n' roll like a junkie, bought tons of records. I would have had long hair, but it never grew far on me, another part of my father's legacy. He was bald as a cue ball.

Sometimes I thought that, because my mother had hit me too many times in the head when I was boy, I might have had some kind of injury. I could follow the words on the page, but after a while the words slipped through the cracks, like trout falling through a net with a hole. My brain felt like that, like it was a net with holes, and whatever went into it came out at the other end. The last whole book I tried to read was a kid's Dr. Seuss book when I was a little boy. One day I was sitting on the front porch of the brownstone, and Murray grabbed it. "Give me back my book," I shouted at him. He threw it off the steps. I ran down the sidewalk to get my book. I heard Murray running behind me. When I bent over to pick it up, Murray stabbed me in the back with a pencil. Between the shoulder blades. Then he broke off the tip. It's still there, in my back. The doctors said it wasn't bad enough for me to worry about lead poisoning.

I wondered what it would be like to be in the world knowing what other people did. I wished that I could read better or understand what I read. Scripture, I believe I understood Scripture. But Ralph has read the entire Bible six times through, and I never even read through it once. I hope the Lord doesn't hold it against me that I never read His Word from front to back. I usually read one passage over and over, trying to understand what it means.

The only thing I knew was my heart. I had a good heart. It wasn't enough to make up for being ignorant, but it was the best I had. Maybe Murray had the airplanes, but God at least had spoken to me. Though I had done many bad things in my life, I always believed that God held me close to his bosom. I tried to walk a close path with the Lord, tried to follow the Word even though I didn't like reading. I tried to be a good husband. A good father. I did the things that I could, like calling the road department for the school bus sign for Gabrielle. Because what if a speeding car turned around the corner and hit her?

Even though I was a simple man, I was still a feeling man. I could feel it when Shelley told me I was nothing, that I was useless, wouldn't amount to nothing. Maybe it was true. But the truth of it didn't erase the hurt of it. If it had been me in her place, I would not have treated my husband like she treated me.

Because I am a big man, strangers sometimes try to pick fights with me. I'll be walking down the sidewalk, and two punks will veer off enough to bump my shoulder. The hunger for a fight comes off them like scent off a deer. If I'm on the bike, an asshole will pull his truck right up to my back tire at the light, or pass me with a slice too close.

One time, when I was still a kid in my twenties, a girl tried to steal my leather jacket in a bar where we both were drinking. I followed her out to the parking lot and grabbed my jacket, saying "You don't ever steal my jacket again." She said, "I thought it was my jacket . . . ," and then her boyfriend came up on the side and punched me in the head. A man that strikes me better make sure I am dead. I grabbed that dude and threw him on the ground and punched him out. I got thrown into the drunk tank. Me thinking, "Moses Unchained," that's my name.

The Scripture says we are to build our houses — meaning our souls — on rock. If you build on sand, the house will crumble. Before I met Shelley, my foundation was rock. But I learned her ways, and her ways shaped me, made me desire what I would not know, made me long for what I would have shunned, made me hate what I wanted to love. I wanted her to love me. I wanted her to think that I was something. On the days she was kind to me, I would have done anything for her without her saying a word, because my heart read her wants. But when she yelled at me, the heart radar shut down, made a wall between me and her that only an open road could comfort.

But she had been kind to me that morning. Her kisses had filled up my empty heart.

And so it was that I put an ad in the newspaper to sell my Harley.

The bike I had built up from parts.

16 On Sunday morning, a man my age with bright, black eyes and a thin face knocked on my door. He wore a leather jacket with a big silver zipper up to the chin, zippers on the pockets and cuffs, and big, black-framed sunglasses.

"I am a walking encyclopedia on Harleys," I told him as we walked around to the yard where I had the bike parked.

"Sure," he said. "How long you had the bike?"

"Four years. I built it from parts. From the ground up."

"It's all from parts?"

I pulled off the cover. He ran his hand over the saddle. It was cherried-out, a 1942 bike, with leather saddlebags and fringe. He ran his hand over the saddle again, more slowly, but while he was feeling, his eyes were scouting every nut. "Can I take a drive?" he asked.

I tossed him my keys. He reached into his jacket pocket and pulled out his set of keys. He threw them to me as he nodded to the truck parked up on the shoulder.

That was him telling me he would not steal my bike.

The Moody Blues were singing "Knights in White Satin" over fourteen speakers full blast. My six pack rested on the porch. I kept the front door open to let out the music that wouldn't get through the screens. Shelley would have shouted me down on two counts, the volume and the open door — it let in flies, she said — but she and Gabrielle were gone to the mall. Every weekend the two of them went to the mall. Every time Shelley left the house, I'd say, "Give me a kiss." Every time she'd screw up her face into a grimace and say, "Right." Sometimes I'd pray that once she would kiss me before I asked the kiss out of her mouth, that she would kiss me willingly.

"Kiss me with the kisses of thy mouth," says the Song of

Solomon. Even though this poem is about a kiss from the Lord, I wanted this kiss from my wife.

At the edge of the property, a weeping willow stood over the stream right before it turned under the road. It was the oldest tree on the land. Its branches overhung the stream and long streamers trailed into the grass and into the water. The willow tree knows the most of all the trees: it is the first green when spring seems far away, and it is the last to lose its leaves in autumn. The willow hangs on to the past season and reaches into the new one. Its branches reminded me of a woman's hair, maybe a mermaid's hair if you could see a mermaid in her natural environment of the water. Her hair would be green and spread out all around in waves.

Around the edge of the stream, the grass had shot up waist-high. One day soon I was going to have somebody bushhog it. A weed eater wasn't strong enough to cut through the weeds with their woody stems and prickly leaves. In the back, the grass was high too. Connecting its stems with the little wires she pulled off a bread bag, Shelley had started to train a rose bush up a trellis on the side wall next to the porch.

If I looked around over my right shoulder, I could see my nearest neighbor if it was winter, but in the spring, the trees blocked my view of his house. His driveway came through my property, but I gave him the right of way. At night, I could see his lights if he had any on, but he could not hear the music from my fourteen speakers.

The music was so loud now — my eyes were shut — that I didn't hear the Harley when the guy — who was Ralph — came down the road. Then the vibrations came into the porch, making the porch vibrate. He rode it up to the porch and took off the helmet, saying, "It's a dream."

"My wife's been on my ass about it."

"I always wanted a classic bike."

He rested in the saddle with his leg slung over it.

"Want a beer?" I asked him.

I tossed him one as he climbed up the steps. The two of us sat on the top step, looking down at the bike, which was parked right in front of us. For a while, neither of us said anything because it was so beautiful, we were locked in admiration. Even though I made it, I still admired it.

Pride goeth before the fall, says the Lord, but this seemed all right.

Finally, the guy said, "My name's Ralph. Ralph Anderson." He had a New Jersey accent.

"Zack. Zack Rosen."

"I'm surprised we haven't met before," Ralph said. "I'd a noticed a bike like that if I saw it."

"I just moved here. With my wife and stepdaughter."

"I got a wife, too. Three kids. Jersey, right?"

"Florida," I told him. "But I grew up in Jersey. Hackensack."

"I knew it." Ralph said. "That accent."

It turns out that he lived in the next town down from me.

"I never thought I'd find someone from Jersey in these hills," I said.

He asked me, "Did you ever see that hearse some guy used to drive around? Main street in Hackensack on a Saturday night. Tinted glass. Remember those surfer's feet stickers? He had two pairs of feet, one on top of the other, like there were two people in the back screwing."

"You saw that hearse?"

"You know it?"

"I owned it. 1961 Cadillac Eureka. Made in Eureka, California. They still make them there. It cost me $400. It had everything. Velvet curtains in the windows. Tinted windshield. It even had the rollers in it. I traded it for two cars. A Cadillac and a

Chevy. I was young and stupid then. I burned them both out. Drove them into the ground and tossed them. That was a long, long time ago. I'm a married man now, thank the Lord."

"You know the Lord?"

"I love the Lord."

"He worked a miracle on me."

■ ■ ■

By the end of the day, I had sold Ralph my Harley. My asking price was $10,000 straight out, but we made a trade. He gave me an old truck that needed its motor rebuilt. He threw in a VCR, and a Jacuzzi that he agreed to put in the bathroom. He also said he would give me help on rebuilding the bannister and would plaster the inside of the house. So even though I didn't make any money on the deal, Ralph was going to help me on the house.

He left before Shelley came home, but she was happy when she heard I got rid of the bike. I didn't tell her that there was hardly any cash attached to it, or that I was getting a half-functional truck in return. I felt so happy about meeting another guy from Jersey, a biker who knew the Lord, that I would have given him the bike on the promise of friendship.

Shelley and Gabrielle came out of the car with two huge shopping bags. Shelley and I went upstairs so Shelley could try on her new dress for me, me carrying the bags.

"Ralph is going to help me with the house," I told her, following her up the stairs.

"Can't you do anything about it in the meantime? String up some rope so nobody falls off the stairs in the middle of the night?"

"I don't have any rope."

"Well, put something up, Zack. It's dangerous. When is this guy — "

"Ralph."

"When he is going to come and work on the house?"

"Pretty soon."

"He took the bike?"

"In his truck."

"He give you a check?"

"He gave me his word. He knows the Lord."

"Zip me up, babe," she said.

It was a purple dress with pleats, belted at the waist.

"You look so good," I told her. "You lost some weight."

"A dress size. I'm down a dress size. What do you think? I have to go to a baby shower next week. Is this all right to wear to a shower?"

"You should be in a beauty pageant. Mrs. Shelley Rosen, Queen for a Day."

She had matching shoes and hose to go with it, and she had spread them all out on the bed. She had to get the shoes, she told me, because she didn't have anything else that matched. This was a woman who was very aware of her appearance. She knew everything about colors and coordination from her painting. When she went to work at the hospital, she was turned out completely, not a hair out of place, lipstick, eye shadow, everything on. She was into her appearance in the way that I had been into the bike. I was truly happy to see my wife so happy.

"Go introduce your dress to the rest of your clothes," I said and popped her on the can.

I went downstairs to the spare bedroom where I used to keep the bike. The dresser was still down there though the bike was gone and I already missed it. I just liked looking at it.

Shelley had started to move all my tools out and fill up the shelves with her books. But all my old Harley parts were still in the dresser. So that morning I sat on the hardwood floor and opened the bottom drawer, seeing what parts I had. An exhaust pipe. Some sprockets and brake handles. A line of cable.

In my old life, I had made the Harley from parts over four years. The first time around, I had started with a taillight. That was it, just a taillight. Then I went to junkyards and found a re-built engine here, some tires there. Piece by piece I had made that thing from parts.

I had so much faith, I could make a new Harley, once again, from the ground up. After all, I had made a new life with my wife. Made it from parts. Baggage, sure she had baggage. The kid. The ex-husband. The bitterness that came with it. But at my age, who didn't have baggage? I had one bad marriage behind me — and Jews marry for life, making that an even more of a count against me. No education. Not much brains. But a path with the Lord. It didn't seem so bad to me.

The willow tree, the tree that knows the most of trees, told me that autumn was a long way off.

When Shelley called me out for supper, asking me to give her a little sugar, I thought that my prayers had finally been answered.

That venereal disease — it was not so hard to forget. It was something in the past.

About a year after I was married, in September 1989, the phone rang, and a man said that he wanted to speak to his mother.

I said, "I think you got the wrong number."

He said, "My mother is Shelley."

I said, "Hold on."

"Shelley," I called to her. "There's someone on the phone for you."

"Who is it?" she asked me, coming down the stairs. She'd been upstairs reading.

"You ask him."

Without changing her features, her face turned white. You could have heard a pin drop in that room.

Sure enough, she had a nineteen-year-old kid she didn't tell me about, Gabrielle's brother, Alex.

When she got off the phone, I asked her, "Do you have any more kids? The dead twins. Alex. How many more kids are going to come out of the woodwork?"

"Zack, you got to understand . . ."

"This is like some crazy movie. Every time I turn around, you got more kids. Some dead. Some living."

"One coming to live with us," she said.

■ ■ ■

I don't think my keeping track of the dates makes me like my father, who still goes on about numbers. I think people keep track of the exact details when they have suffered a trauma in life. Everything before the trauma suddenly becomes clear. All the signs were there in advance, and you can't see them at the time, but after, they looked so obvious. In my mind, I keep going over the dates, the events, because I keep looking for the place where I might have done something differently. But I didn't know. I just didn't know. If you are ignorant, signs don't mean anything. It's just one thing in a life where other things happen. No one event stands out. But after the event, they all stand out like they were written in red letters twenty-feet high, and you have to wonder: how did I miss it?

■ ■ ■

Two weeks later, on October 11, 1989, Alex moved in with us. He was a skinny kid, still with acne, but he ate like a horse. His hair was down to his shoulders. He wore thick-soled, high-topped tennis shoes that made him walk around like a puppy with feet too big for its body. Shelley gave Alex the Harley room, which now, since there was no more Harley, accommodated him. When he came, he brought one navy-blue duffle bag. He didn't have a driver's license until I took him for one, and he didn't have a car, so Shelley picked him up from the Trailways bus station.

The kid couldn't get a job. Shelley said he'd leave the house in the morning with a newspaper and come back in the afternoon with hamburger wrappers stuck to the bottom of his shoes. Alex and Gabrielle got along all right, though. When I saw the two of them together on days I didn't leave for work at the crack of dawn, they'd be out watching crickets or grasshoppers in the tall grass in the back. Sometimes, they'd leave their muddy shoes on the back steps to the laundry room after they'd been swimming in the stream. A little bit upstream, where the mill used to have been, was once a dam. Now most of the blocks are down, but part of the wall remains standing; the water comes over that wall and falls into a pool below, so it's possible to swim in that water hole.

I got Alex a car, but he was very unhappy. He didn't fit in here. He was a big kid, way bigger than me, with a good heart. I worked him. I needed a lot of work done at the house, work that didn't need education just common sense. When he wasn't out looking for work, I had a list of things for him to do. I made lists for him like I now make lists for Ralph. I must be a list-making kind of person. But I was clear about myself. I knew what I expected from people, and I told them. I was always real clear.

If I had been more discerning, I might have discovered the truth about Shelley, but I always believed her. She was my wife — I was *supposed* to trust her. When I looked for the meaning of anything, I looked for the revealed meaning of God. I looked to see the hand of God in the signs I saw. A car wreck — God's hand was in it. Winning the lottery — God's will. I didn't need to know more than that. What happened was the will of God. Period. If God didn't will it to happen, it wouldn't have happened; therefore, God caused what was.

Someone once gave me a pamphlet put out by the "Radio Bible Series," the same series I listened to in the truck. "How Can I Know Who To Marry?" was the title. I had carried that pamphlet around in my back pocket and read parts of it over a month.

I had followed all the steps.

There were five steps to choosing a spouse: 1) Choose a believer. 2) Trust God. 3) Consider character. 4) Use wisdom. 5) Think ahead.

1) I chose a believer.

We met in church. Furthermore, she was a Leviticus Jewish woman converted to Christianity.

2) Trust God.

The pamphlet said, "We Christians have to learn patience." I had prayed for two years. Waited two years. Chaste for two years. It seemed like patience to me.

3) On character, it said, "Would you want a heart surgeon who was a regular user of cocaine, a psychopathic killer, or a medical intern who had cheated his way through medical school? So, too, you need to be sure that person you choose to marry has the right qualifications to be your husband or wife."

I made a mistake on number three. I didn't know Shelley well enough. And there's another thing. What do you do when the person lies?

On number four, I messed up too. It said, "Don't base your decision on one sign."

I did. But it was a big sign. Meeting a Leviticus Jew in a Baptist church? Seems like the size of the sign should count for something. Which is better, one big clear sign, like a neon arrow pointing down from heaven at the woman's head, saying, "This is it," or signs so small you need a microscope to see them?

∎ ∎ ∎

The day before Alex came on the bus, Shelley was in the Harley room with a trash can. She was going through my dresser with the Harley parts, ready to throw them all out. I watched her do it. Then she dragged the bag to the front porch for me to carry the trash to the dump. No way, I thought, this woman is going to make me carry my own Harley parts to the dump.

When she went to cook dinner, I took the bag off the porch and hid it in the cellar.

∎ ∎ ∎

I got back things people wanted to throw out. Like with Shelley's book. Ralph tossed it in with the pot plants, but I reached in again and pulled it out. Every book he pulled off the shelf, I put back.

"Everything that was her, it's in those books," I told him.

He closed up the trash bag and dragged it out on the porch so that one of us would take it to the dump.

Even now, parts of the house still feel like they are her body. Like the books. She had put them up in the shelves in her precise order. She had arranged them, written in some, never turned a page in others. She had composed them in a series.

In the Harley room, with the bookshelves and the books, in the room that is now Ralph's room, I used to feel Shelley's presence like a ghost. Ralph was the only one I knew who had enough spirit to sleep in that room. The hand of God had touched him. It made him immune to evil. Even though he is sleeping with Patrice and leaving his wife, his heart is sound in his breast. His goodness makes a shield that comes between me and the ghost of my wife. Thank the Lord.

In early fall I had Alex out in the yard breaking ground for bulbs. I had a vision of tulips coming up everywhere in the yard. Tulips and crocus. Sometimes an iris will send its purple spears up through the snow. It knows when to bloom. When it blooms through the snow, you know spring is on the way.

I went back to the porch for a cup of coffee Shelley had brought out to me. She watched her son turn up the soil. He was covered head to foot in my old clothes. My flannel hat with the flaps coming down off his ears. My jacket with the fur collar pulled up over the ear flaps. My gloves on his hand. Steam of his breath surrounded him.

"When I die," Shelley said, "I want to be buried in the yard."

"What are you talking about dying for?"

"Promise me. Promise me, Zack, that when I die you will bury me in the yard."

"I promise," I told her, "but you aren't going anywhere without me, baby."

"I won't leave you," she told me.

I said, "Fine. I want to talk to you about something."

She said, "Talk."

"I want to adopt Gabrielle. I think she should have a real father."

She said, "No way."

"Do you want a new father?" Shelley called through the house to Gabrielle. Gabrielle said nothing back.

Afterward, the lawyer who wrote up Shelley's will told me she had come to him. She told him, "Something terrible has happened. I want a divorce."

But she didn't tell him what happened.

I asked Shelley if she would get marriage counseling with me.

She wouldn't, but she said we should look for a home church. We went around to several churches. She liked the New Valley Baptist Church, where we met with Pastor Buttersmith who wore a tie and was very polite. In the church, he had given a rousing testimony about the work the church did in Africa. The main pastor, Joseph Elder, was going to go to Africa to do the work of the Lord. All of those children starving in Ethiopia lived without the Word. Then he asked for a second collection for the building fund.

My favorite church was a little cinder-block place in a small town thirty miles away. The pastor there, Johnny, had a sixth-grade education, but he owned a construction business he had built up himself. He owned three hundred head of cattle, and he had built the church on his own property. Every block in it had been carried and laid by Johnny's hands or by the hands of someone in his congregation. On Saturdays, he went to the prisons to give inmates the Word. I don't know when Johnny slept. Anybody hurting, he was there. He had the marks of the Lord's prosperity on him, and he was a plain-speaking man, a hard-speaking man. I learned about this church from Ralph and Marianne when they were still married.

Ralph was a deacon in this church, but Marianne left it before he did. One time, Johnny had said something about "crying like a woman" or the "chatter of women." Marianne said he was a sexist preacher, coming down on women. So she left and went to New Valley, where she complained to Pastor Elder and Pastor Buttersmith about Johnny's sexist comments on women. They both humiliated Johnny publicly about that, saying things like he was a country preacher.

I understood Marianne's point of view. It wasn't the women per se that he was down on. Johnny did not believe that women told lies by nature. It was something that was in the Bible, a kind of catchy phrase: "the chatter of women." But considering the kind of lies I heard from Shelley, I thought there must be some truth in the biblical side, though my reasoning mind tells me that Shelley was crazy and that her craziness had nothing to do with her sex. It wasn't the chatter of women; it was the chatter of madness. That is the noise it makes. Disorganized noise, pointless noise. Random. Noise without meaning. Having its own meaning like speaking in tongues. Needing interpretation.

I wonder if that was what Sateen meant. The loon.

■ ■ ■

I helped Alex get into the air force in March 1990. Five months after Alex joined the air force, he came home on leave. He looked good. His hair was cut short, and he was beginning to have a man's face. His mother wasn't home yet, but we drank a cup of tea together, and he said, "Where's my lists?"

I said I didn't make lists for any recruit but asked him if he wanted to walk around the property. He had bushhogged the deep grass by the stream, and it looked good. He had helped me build up the shed, and I had given it a new coat of paint. He had turned up the earth in the back, and I had planted some flowers. So I said, "Let's go look at the flowers you helped plant."

We were out walking on my property when I saw a police car pull into the driveway. I watched to see if it would turn around in the driveway, but it came straight up to the porch.

"Is there anything I should know?" I asked Alex. "Are you AWOL?"

He said no.

I walked up to the sheriff with Alex trailing a few feet behind me. The sheriff climbed out of his car. This was in August of 1990.

I had asked my wife at least a hundred times — after her nineteen-year-old son showed up — if she only had two children. I must have asked her a hundred times, "Do you have any more kids?"

She said, "No. Will you leave me alone and stop asking me?"

My trust factor with her was low. Skeletons in the closet were constantly coming out. I asked her so many times, she said "Would you leave me alone?" So I stopped with that.

Then the sheriff came up to me. "I am looking for Shelley Moffat," he said. "Does she live here?"

I said, "She does. She's not here. What is this in reference to?" I asked him.

He said, "This is a private matter. I got to serve papers on her."

I said to him, "There's no way you're leaving here without telling me. This is my married wife. This is my property. I understand you want to serve papers, but can you tell me what this is about?"

He said, "This is in reference to child support for Daniel and Arthur Scoobie."

I turned to Alex, "What is this about?"

The boy's face turned red as a tomato. He said, "You need to talk to my mother, that's all I know."

I called her up at work.

I said, "Your twins that died have just risen from the grave."

She knew all the time.

She had eleven-year-old twins who were living in New York state with a man she had married, whom she never told me about. When you get married in the state of Florida, you are supposed to list the number of previous marriages. Shelley had written "one," but she had at least two. She had denied that marriage and lied on the certificate and never even privately acknowledged that to me. I had no idea. I had just found out about the twin sons she had and the marriage I didn't know about. This man I didn't know was suing me for child support for kids she didn't even say she had.

When I married the woman, I thought she had one ten-year-old kid. I found out that she had four children. That wasn't the end of it.

When we were still in Florida and deciding where to start our new life, Shelley had a map, an atlas. She had a place circled in red, a place in upstate New York. The place where she wanted to move — where we never arrived — was where those twins were. I didn't know that at the time. But that's why we had headed north rather than west. I understood it later. Mexico or New Mexico — it was all the same. They were both places I would never see.

At Thanksgiving, Shelley yelled at me because I waited to load the dishwasher. I said, "Can't you wait until our company goes?" She was screaming at me so loud, everyone could hear it through the house.

Ralph came into the kitchen, put his arm around my shoulder, and said low in my ear, "Listen, buddy, we got to go."

I grabbed his arm and said, "Please, don't leave me, Ralph."

So Ralph and I went out to the porch, and I asked him how the bike was running. He said it ran great. He said I was a genius with that bike.

"There's one thing, Zack, I wanted to tell you about."

"Anything for you Ralph."

"I changed the color. I always wanted the classic color, red. So I had it painted."

I told him, "Anything you do is great. It's your bike anyhow, Ralph."

"I know. I wanted to tell you gently. It's Thanksgiving. I know you love that bike."

He lit up a Camel, sucking up the smoke deeply.

"I'm thinking of leaving Marianne," he said softly, his eyes squeezed together, his voice very soft.

"No way, Ralph," I said, checking over my shoulder that the front door was shut.

"I just can't go on. She makes lists. Lists of things for me to do. She's always on my case."

"But that's a normal part of married life," I said. "The change. All that stuff."

"We don't sleep together in the bed, Zack. We haven't for some months."

We both fell silent. I said, "That's all Shelley and I do. Sex."

"When I got married, I got married for life," Ralph said. "I understood what marriage was, what the rules were. But I don't love my wife. A taskmaster is all she is. I feel like a slave. Do this, do that. No loving."

"With Shelley, I thought I married one person, and she turned out to be a different person. I was always the same person, Ralph. A dumb-ass working-class man."

"I'll never forget that day. 'Your twins have returned from the grave.'" He laughed with a kind of howl. It seemed like a wild howl, but really it was an ironic howl.

Sometimes the two of us sat on the porch bench and laughed and howled. We howled at the irony that bent the spokes of our lives. We howled from the wonderment that we were such fools. Our lives, we thought, were together. But we had been blind-sided into thinking everything was all right. Neither of us had wanted that much from life. Steady job. A family. Kids. A nice wife. It did not seem so much. We could not believe the way that our lives had turned out so differently from what we expected. Two dumb-ass pussy-whipped working men. Hen-pecked and miserable. We couldn't believe it was us in these lives, and so we had the wonderment that you'd have looking at the Grand Canyon. From the north rim, the canyon stretches out so far below and the sky stretches so far above, it puts you in a state of disbelief that anything like that could exist. That was the size of our wonderment.

A normal life — it seemed like everything.

Marianne was frowning when she cracked the screen door open. "Ralph, it's time to go," she said through the crack.

"It's a screen door," Ralph said. "Why does she have to open a screen door to speak to me? She could talk through the door, that's what screens are for."

"She just wanted you to know, I guess," I said.

"Know what?"

"That she meant it enough to open the door."

When Marianne came out for good, she had a little brown bag packed up with leftovers. She carried it like it was a purse held up against her chest. Her dress had a little lace collar. Marianne was flat-chested with spindly legs, her hair cut square around her face. She snatched Ralph by the shoulder and pulled him out to the car, waving good-bye to me in the meantime.

Shelley was waiting for me inside. "So, you let the women do the dishes? You men eat like pigs and let the women clean up. What a fucking pig."

"Baby," I said, "it's Thanksgiving. Can't we have a little peace?"

"Peace for you but not for me."

"You shoulda came and got me."

"You been sneaking to Johnny's church? Is that where you and Ralph go? Listening to Johnny down women?"

"Leave Johnny out of this," I told her. "He's practically a father to me."

"Son of a bitch," she said. Then she looked at me coldly, with something like hate in her eyes. "Four years," she said.

"What do you mean four years? Is that how long our marriage is going to last? Are you going to leave me after four years?"

She laughed at me. She said, "You're really going to miss me when I am gone."

I said, "Yeah," but I was thinking to myself, "Where are you going? I'm not divorcing you. I want to be with you."

 When Alex came, he had brought Gabrielle some rabbits. He came home with four bunnies and built them a rabbit cage of chicken wire and wood, which he put out on the side of the house.

"The greenest part of the yard," he told me, "is going to be under that rabbit cage."

To this day, I still don't know what kids like about rabbits. Rabbits are furry and warm to the touch, but they don't do much. They wiggle their noses and crap on the floor. Sometimes Gabrielle would bring them in the house where they struggled to get behind the sofa. If the door shut suddenly, the bunnies hopped wildly with legs scratching on the carpet. Then it would take both Alex and Gabrielle to catch one bunny and cage it.

■ ■ ■

I used to hate the calls that said it was time to take a load across the valley. On hauls like that, I'd have to drive five hundred miles in a day, deliver a load of cardboard, then turn round and come back the next day. I'd be sipping coffee, singing, playing the radio, driving on those hauls alone, listening to the radio and thinking about the Lord. I wondered why He gave me this to live with in my life — these two children and the invisible twins who I never saw but who became a part of my life because they were a part of Shelley's life. But Sunday was coming up, the Lord's day, and I could go to church, see Ralph and my pastor, Johnny, and I got more comfort from the church than I got at home.

Shelley was awake ahead of me walking around the house in a white bathrobe and making coffee. I could smell the coffee even from the upstairs with the covers pulled up to my chin. I came down the stairs. At the bottom of stairs lay a scattering of rabbit droppings.

At the kitchen table, Shelley sat reading the newspaper, drinking a cup of coffee. She still had a cold and wiped her nose with a napkin. Her feet were bare and dark on the bottom. I wished she had washed her feet or worn slippers.

I poured myself a cup in my "Jews for Jesus" mug.

"You want to go to church with me?" I asked Shelley.

"No," she said still reading the newspaper.

"Anything wrong?" I asked her.

"No," she said, not looking up.

"You haven't gone to church with me in a month," I told her. I liked to keep church-going regular, and I liked to go with my wife.

"Are you going to keep on my ass about church?" she asked me. "I'd like to know if you are. Because if you keep on my ass, I will just go upstairs now and go back to bed. I'd rather avoid the whole thing than listen to you on my ass."

"I'm not on your ass," I said.

"Hell you're not."

"I am too tired to fight," I said.

She got up and snatched the newspaper off the table. "I am going back to bed. I have a cold."

"If you see Gabrielle, tell her to clean up the rabbit shit. Rabbit shit in the house."

"Rabbit shit and your shit. If we had a decent house, we wouldn't be living in rabbit shit. You tell her. She's in her room."

"Did you step in that rabbit shit?"

I turned my back on her and poured myself another cup of coffee. I could feel her eyes, like ice picks, chipping away at my back. It made my back ache in the old place, where Dr. Mary Dolor used to rub the heel of her hand.

My first wife shot up my Harley. I got two rich brothers who scorn me, a mother who beat me till the County heard me scream, a father in and out of mental institutions. I went to the pain doctor who did not doctor my pain. And now I got a crazy wife who stabs me with her eyes. With skeletons coming out of the closet right and left.

It might have been funny if it didn't hurt so much.

You dumb Jewish truck driver, that's what she said to me in so many words.

"Look at me when I talk to you," she said.

I kept pouring my coffee, trying to make a soundproof wall around me so I couldn't hear her. A glorious Sunday — I longed for the peace of the morning.

On the first day, it must have been like this, with the land separated from the firmament, with the light streaming down to the earth in waves like golden hair. On the day that God made Adam, it must have been good like this, with Adam going around and naming the things in his garden. Life must have changed for the better when God made Eve because Eve was a helpmeet and was loving of her man. It did not seem too much to ask for, that a woman love the man who loves her. I would never leave her, and she knew it. I wouldn't let her go, and she hated me for it. But I had made the promise: till death do us part.

Shelley came up behind me and grabbed my hand while I was pouring coffee. I poured hot coffee all over my hand, the heel of my thumb and half my inner hand throbbing red with steam coming off.

"Son of a bitch," I said. "Let go."

I shook her off my arm, which she had grabbed ahold of, her saying, "Look at me. Look at me, motherfucker."

I flung my arm backward to shake her off, saying, "Go take some aspirin." I shook her off, ran cold water in the sink, and put my scalded hand in it. Even under the clear stream of spring water, my hand shone red. I was going to have to tape it up when I went on the road again — maybe get some gauze and Noxema to take the sting out. It throbbed like a drum even under the faucet.

"Is there any Noxema in the house?" I asked.

Shelley didn't say anything. I broke off a leaf from an aloe plant over the sink and squeezed the juice onto my hand. In the cutlery drawer, I found a steak knife to split the aloe leaf length-wise, opening it to cover more of my hand. Then I threw the knife in the sink.

When I turned around to look at Shelley, it wasn't because I wanted to look her but it was because I had the feeling Shelley might creep up on me when I wasn't looking. It was just a feeling.

When I turned around, she didn't have a knife. She stood across the kitchen, rage sending lightning out of her eyes.

"I didn't bring the rabbits into the house. You tell Gabrielle," she said.

"She's your daughter," I said.

"Some father you are. You good-for-nothing. Shirking the re-sponsibilities of fatherhood."

"Is that why you never told me about the twins?"

"Fuck you," she said, and started up the stairs into the bedroom.

By then I was fuming mad, my hand hurt, and I was frustrated at not having any peace in my own house. I followed her up the stairs.

"Do you have any more children?" I asked her back, the heels of her feet practically kicking me in the face. "You dirty-feeted woman. Where are your other kids?"

She ran up as fast as she could. By the time I got to the bedroom, she was throwing clothes off the hangers onto the bed. "I'm leaving. You good-for-nothing son of a bitch. You'll never amount to anything. I don't know why I ever married you. Slippers, you want slippers, fine. Fuck you."

She hauled out a pair of fuzzy woolen slippers shaped like bear claws and threw them at me.

"Let me help you," I said. "You want to leave, fine."

I went past her and grabbed an armful of dresses and threw them on the bed. When I came back for a second load, Shelley grabbed my arm and dug her fingernails into my skin. Her nails slid down to the scalded spot. "Get your hands off my clothes," she said.

I did. She was on my arm, and she scared me with that rage so I hit her with my hand. I hit her on the eye. It did not break the skin, or bruise, or anything, but I had hit her.

"That does it," she said, looking at me, stunned.

"A man doesn't hit once," she said. "A man that hits once will hit again."

She grabbed some clothes, went into the bathroom, and locked the door.

I went back downstairs. Gabrielle was playing music in her bedroom with the door closed, but I had the feeling she was listening to us.

In the laundry room, I found a clean pair of jeans and got dressed from clothes in the dryer. I pulled my boots over my jeans. Then I went out to the yard to walk the edge of my property. That was the first and only time I ever hit her.

That became her new thing. I hit her. Me, a two hundred–

pound trucker. Hit his petite wife in the eye. When she had a cold.

That was the first time she left the house to file a police report. Before she beat me over the head with the umbrella.

I walked through the tall grass by the stream, pulled off my boots, and jumped into the stream.

The current was swift for the size of it. From the surface, it looked like a gentle brook, but the force cut my knees out from under me. The water comes down the mountain, comes from rain, comes from snow. It pulled me around and deeper into it. I lay back and stretched with my feet anchoring me at the bottom.

I longed for desert places then. The flat plain of New Mexico with stretches of sky, clear-blue sky and dry desert air. I wanted to breathe some air that didn't have damp in it, that had something in it that was bare. I imagined New Mexico as a place where the landscape was stripped down, like a motor mount. Where the colors were simple, blue and brown. Where the sky was filled with quiet and peace, peace enough to hear God speaking. Where there weren't children coming out from everywhere.

The dirt and gravel from the stream bottom drifted into my socks, and I half-floated for half an hour with my heels dragging on the stream bed. I imagined myself as a deer might see me. Coming down to drink, cracking twigs, nosing through the grass, the deer would see a white form, like a log, like a crocodile, drifting back and forth, anchored by legs, with eyes shut against the sky.

I swam to the edge of the creek and pulled myself out with both hands. I lay down in the tall grass, and it made a hedge around me. The sky above was clear and blue. A white streak from a jet's vapor trail left the only mark on that sky. I wished for clouds and thunder and lightning.

I believed myself to be a good man, and yet I had hit a woman. I was not the kind of man to do a thing like that. I had been hit enough as a child. It hurt me to give pain to anything. But Shelley made me afraid that I might do it again. And though maybe I wasn't the kind of man who did things like that, she was making me into the kind of man that I was not.

What went wrong?

What was my kind of man?

I was the kind of man who liked to walk close to God. I was happiest with the simple things. A rear light to a motorcycle, motorcycle parts, things I could do with my hands made me happy. I wished for Ralph then, for him and me to sit on the porch and howl at the absurdity of our lives. I didn't understand why my wife hated me so. I was good to her. I was kind to her daughter. Anything she wanted I did. Sure I had the bike. A man has got to have something in his life. But then, I even gave up the bike. I did everything I could to make her happy. We made a new life. It was in my blood to be married — in me as a Jew and as a Christian. But I didn't know how to fix anything. Before my very eyes, I was turning into a monster.

I lay down in the grass and wept like a woman.

 In spring of 1991, Shelley was sick off and on with colds though I didn't see much of it. She cut down on her hours at work. She was a heart nurse, best buddies with other doctors and nurses, so she told them she wanted to cut down on her hours. She had flex time and worked one or two days a week. The idea was this: the less money she made, the less she had to pay for the twin's child support. Meanwhile, we were going broke. My income paid for

the house and the food, but Shelley loved to buy new clothes, new furniture, new everything. She applied for credit cards in both our names and ran them up to the max. She had more silk dresses than the Queen of the Philippines. When our credit reached the limit, she would buy a new dress, wear it once and take it back, go screaming to the clerk that it had a hole in it or a run in the silk. Once I saw her ruin a red dress by making a snag in the skirt with a nail. Then she gave the clerk high hell for it. It ruined our evening. One minute the three of us were walking through the mall holding hands like a family. The next minute she was yelling at the girl.

We declared bankruptcy.

■ ■ ■

Ralph came over to work on the plastering. He had a drop cloth in the white room and a ladder, and he was standing on the ladder. I came in the room and asked if he wanted a drink of water.

"Yeah, I could use a break," he said.

Shelley wasn't home. She had a doctor's appointment, she told me. The doctor had called saying she had a little spot on her lung during her annual examination.

Ralph and I strung up a spare extension cord through the columns of the bannister; it didn't have a handrail yet.

"Johnny asked about you," Ralph said. "You haven't been faithful to the church."

Ralph was still a deacon. After he left Marianne, he resigned. But back then, he was a deacon.

"I'm getting my heart right," I told him.

"Pretty tough stuff, eh? The twins. Alex."

I didn't say anything.

When Shelley came home, she went into the kitchen.

"How was the doctor's?" I called to her.

"I didn't go," she said.

She had just gone to buy aspirin.

The rest of the week, she was very ill. She had a fever and had a hard time breathing. She panted like she did the night she told me about the twins. It was on a Thursday. I brought her to the doctor, and it looked like her lungs were all filled up. The doctor said he would do a CAT scan the following Monday. That day Shelley grew sicker, needed medicine. I worked only half a day, brought medicine home to her. Saturday and Sunday she was very sick, stayed in the house. Shelley was, when I met her, an extremely attractive woman, 155 pounds of woman that was very Rubenesque, large-busted but not heavy. At this point, she was 115 pounds, as thin as she could get without looking bad. Still, she looked perfect at that weight.

The weekend went by. Sunday she slept like a rock. Her uncle called, the one who owned the house in Florida. She said for me to hand her the phone, but she was so weak, she could barely hold it, so I held it for her, cupped up under her chin.

"I am the sickest I have ever been in my life," she told him. "I want you to know that I love you and care about you."

"Shelley, you need to get to a doctor," I kept telling her.

"Leave me alone," she said.

That night she slept like a baby. She didn't breathe heavily. Morning came. As soon as she woke, she had a hard time breathing. Her lips had turned blue. She breathed like a dog in the summertime panting for a drink of water. I called Dr. Phillips and told him that I was bringing her to the emergency room at the hospital and that he should meet us there. At the time he thought I was hysterical, but I wasn't. He insisted that I bring her to his office first. He had no idea she was as sick as she was.

I dressed her. I grabbed a pair of panties. I put her bra on her. Her blouse didn't match her pants. Knowing her, I thought she would give me a real hard time. But she didn't care. We were still using the extension cord, strung up on the outside of the stairs, as a bannister, so I helped her down the stairs. I got her to her car, and she just plopped in. She was totally conscious and awake. To the doctor's office, it's a ten-mile stretch on the Parkway. She was totally conscious, she had her eyes open, she had an opportunity to talk to me, but she didn't say a word. She just watched me. Sometimes she closed her eyes together tightly.

I drove her to the doctor's office. Dr. Phillips got a wheelchair, brought her in, and administered oxygen. Instantly he realized that something was seriously wrong with her vital signs. Someone called the ambulance because two or three minutes after she was there this man came to transfer her and took her into the ambulance. I wasn't allowed to go in the back of the ambulance with her, so I drove. It was raining that Monday. This was about ten or eleven in the morning. They brought her into the emergency room. The doctors were working on her. They came out and began asking me questions.

They asked me: "Do you use bug spray? Do you use chemicals?" Was she breathing this? Was she doing that? Was she doing this? I couldn't understand what their concern was.

Because she was an RN heart nurse, in charge of scheduling the other nurses, she was one of their own at the city hospital. While the doctors were asking me questions, there were people going in and out of the ER. I saw the door open; there were five or seven doctors working on her. They had had a hospital robe on her initially, but when I saw her she was totally naked, on a table tilted at a 45-degree angle. I literally saw one doctor looking in her eyes as another doctor — one at either end — was looking into each of her ears, while another doctor was on his knees or squatting with a flashlight and rubber gloves with his hands in her vagina looking in there all around.

"What is going on?" I asked but no one told me anything.

Time passed, maybe two minutes. The door to the ER unit was the kind that opened and closed slowly, on a pump. Two minutes after I saw that scene, someone else went into that ER room, and the door opened all the way; it closed very slowly. In the space of that closing, my wife and I had eye contact for the last time. I didn't know it then, but what she was saying was, "This is it. I'm dying. It's all over. Today you will know the whole truth."

I didn't know she was dying then. I can still see the door closing very slowly the last time we made eye contact. It was eleven o'clock in the morning. An hour or so later, they moved her upstairs to the ICU, to the ward on the seventh floor; she worked on the sixth floor. They fed me a free lunch downstairs. A bologna sandwich on white bread with tea.

Shelley had a real hard time breathing. Two o'clock came around and one of the RNs asked me if I wanted to see my wife. Two o'clock was visiting hours, and I could see her for twenty minutes. I thought it would be great: they would have her on an IV and be feeding her through a bottle and have oxygen to her. She must have been doing good enough for me to see her.

They should never have let me in there.

They had an IV bottle, not stuck into her arm, but in a vein in her neck because they couldn't find a vein her body: they were feeding her intravenously through her neck. She didn't have the standard oxygen mask on; she had a tube down her throat that was connected to a machine that looked like an accordion that pumped oxygen down her lungs. Her stomach moved up and down like waves. You could see it as the machine was working, her stomach was moving back and forth. One of the fingers was bleeding under the nail. All her fingers and toes had turned blue. The human body knows to let the oxygen go to the organs.

The nurses should never have let me go in there. They had given her some kind of injections and hooked her up to a respirator.

After that, about 2:15 or 2:30, I went back to the waiting room. There was a woman in there who said, "You don't have any family? There is no one else you could call?"

I let a little time go by. At four o'clock, someone called the code blue. I still had no idea what was happening. When the code blue came, people from all floors came up with all different apparatus. I said it couldn't be her, but it was her. Her heart stopped. They jump-started it one or two times. She had a cardiac arrest. And that's what happened. I called Ralph, and he came.

A pastor was there, Pastor Buttersmith from New Valley. As I was sitting in there, he walked past. I called to him: "Pastor." He looked in. I told him that my wife was in there and she was dying. He told me to calm down, that I was not realistic, that just because people go into ICU they're not dying.

I said, "Look, my wife's heart just stopped. They got it started again. But she's in there dying."

He thought I was crazy and not realistic.

I called my mom before Shelley went to ICU. My mother told me to chill out, that nobody dies of pneumonia.

The pastor stood with me to the last hour of her life.

Dr. Phillips came out, took me aside, and said, "Zack, I want to do an AIDS test on Shelley."

All I knew about was homosexuality.

I said, "Fine. Do what you got to do."

They took her blood, but the results didn't come back until six days later. She died at 4:55 that afternoon. She was with the Lord. The whole thing happened in seven hours, and I had no idea what happened. It unraveled right in front of me. She was forty-three years old, the mother of four children. She had been an RN heart nurse for twenty years.

When Ralph finally came in, I hugged him and said, "She's with the Lord, Ralph."

∎ ∎ ∎

As that door was closing the last time I saw her, she opened her mouth and what I saw shocked me. She had the worst case of thrush I have ever seen. Her mouth was infected totally through, and I'm sure into her esophagus. What killed her was not the water in her lungs. She was consumed by the parasites in her own body.

My wife. My married wife.

Twenty-four hours after Shelley's death, her mother and half-brother came to claim the body. They went through the house and took all Shelley's good things, her jewelry, her china, her family belongings. They took Gabrielle with them. They flew to New Jersey. My mother stayed with me on Friday. She went through the house and found all different kinds of papers.

"What's this?" Mabel asked me, holding up a life insurance policy. "Did you know this, Zack?" she asked me.

I vaguely remembered something about the policy, but Shelley was always telling me things that I could not follow. And now that she was dead, I couldn't follow anything at all. But Mabel said, "Look at this. Shelley changed the will."

In the event that both of us were killed, the house would go to her daughter. I thought this was strange, a special policy that both of us would die together? I thought to myself: "What is this? Was she planning on killing me?"

I couldn't understand it. My mother was upset and bewildered. She never liked Shelley to begin with; my mother suggested that I get tested from the top of my head to the bottom of my feet. So I had Dr. Phillips test me for everything before Ralph and me flew to New Jersey for the funeral. Saturday evening at the wake, her half-brother came up to me and said, "Shelley died of pneumonia."

When I came back to Virginia, I got a call from Dr. Phillips to come into his office. Usually I am late for everything. This time I was on time. When I came into his office, I sat in his office chair. He knew Shelley from the hospital. I used to come for my physical, and we would quote Scripture. Dr. Phillips had known us the whole time we were in Virginia. He knew the Lord.

I asked him, "Is it AIDS?"

All he said was, "I am sorry."

I went from having a family to no family in one week. I learned about the betrayal. My wife died of AIDS, and I was infected. With all of that on my shoulders, I'm in a house by myself. Everywhere I look, I see my wife. I have to go back to work and drive a ninety thousand–pound tanker truck, an eighteen-wheeler, and function at full capacity.

One day while I'm driving down the road, both my hands start shaking. My teeth chatter. I gasp for breath. I can't do this any-more. I am medically disabled.

■■■

My crazy father bushwhacked me on the phone before I started screening my messages. "Sonny, what got into you? Why did you marry that woman? She had eight children. Couldn't you just have slept with her? You married her."

"Dad," I said, "that was twenty years ago."

He was stuck in time. "Eight children."

That was Frieda. He never got over that.

"How's your mother? She doing all right? You talk to her, you tell her Sal loves her."

"I'll tell her. You love her."

"She still in Florida?"

"Yes. Same house."

"God bless her."

Mom had moved back to New Jersey with her boyfriend, but she told me, "You tell Sal where I am, I'll kill you." She was afraid Sal would come to her house with flowers and significant num-bers. They had been apart thirty years. He still thought he had a chance with her.

"You know this thing you got, Zack," he continued. "People live a long time with it."

"I know. Good-bye, Dad."

"Health problems a'ready. Who doesn't have them?"

People go for years.

The cure was on the way.

I could have a normal working life until . . .

Everything would be just the same as normal until . . .

■■■

In Shelley's papers I found a picture of her husband. The last one. David. The spitting image of that guy on the curb in Jensen

Beach. She had told me David lived in Miami. The truth was he lived two blocks away from her Uncle Evan's house. She left a taped message to Gabrielle. There wasn't much to it but things like "I love you." She hadn't left anything for me.

The Florida number I dialed from her book put me in touch with David's father. "Your son was married to Shelley Sondheim?" I asked him.

"Yes," he said.

"Shelley is dead from AIDS," I told him.

"So what?"

"Tell your son to get tested," I said.

"He's dead already."

"He gave it to her?"

He hung up on me.

■ ■ ■

I counted time backward. She talked about the insurance. I got that venereal disease. Those things went together. I fell off the catwalk. Had neuropathy in my legs. Diarrhea. She never left me and Gabrielle alone together; she must have thought Gabrielle would say something. She even quit her job in Florida to make sure that I wouldn't be alone with the child. She must have known she had infected me. She changed the policy when she knew she'd infected me. She wanted me to screw her in the ass. When she had her period. *That's my blood* her saying to me about the sheets. *Four years* meaning "that's all the time you'll have." *David ruined my life* not meaning a metaphor. *Bury me in the yard* and *death always finds me.*

When I'm gone, when I'm gone, when I'm gone . . .

You're sure going to miss me when I'm gone . . .

■ ■ ■

I sat on the sofa in the dark with the television off. An alarm clock on the coffee table ticked off the minutes. At first I set the clock for the hour. Every hour the alarm went off. I shut it off. I wanted every hour. Measured every hour. With every tick, I told myself, "I'm still not dead." After a day, I turned on the television. Measured time by television shows. The morning news. The morning talk shows. The noon news. The afternoon talk shows. I kept expecting I would die. I listened to my heart and wondered why it sounded so steady. I looked around the house, and my eyes saw the world the same way that they used to. My ears heard the same way. I could speak in the same way. But everything looked different.

Four years. Four years. Four years. Four years.

■ ■ ■

I did not leave the house for four months. I went to bed on the sofa and did not leave the house. I sat in the dark with the TV on. I watched TV all day, and I watched TV all night. Any minute, I was going to die.

Sprocket. Cylinder. Cable. PTO. Power take-off. Press the button so you can move the dumpster on the dump truck. Trolley brake. Hydraulic brake. Four-wheel drive. Overhead cam. Dual exhaust. Intake manifold. Outtake manifold.

Biker words.

Trucker words.

There are no pain words.

■ ■ ■

My brother Frankie calling, saying, "People can go for a long time."

I watched the Geraldo show so often, I called the "Speak-Up" number. A producer called me back to be on an HIV show. When the producer told me I'd be on the air with hookers, I said no.

But I had told my mother about Geraldo, and she had told Murray, and Murray told me: "I've got some big deals in the pipeline. Don't use the family name, Zack."

■ ■ ■

I didn't leave the house for four months except for chores. I couldn't eat.

Everyplace I looked in the house, I saw Shelley. Some people from the church came and took her dresses and feminine things that Gabrielle did not get. That was a blessing in itself. I could not touch anything. Her clothes were everywhere, but now they were just clothes. Her underwear. She had a sexy underwear drawer. She had lots of shoes. Makeup. All those parts of her lost their meaning without her. This house had been remade for her, the yard planted for her, my labor given to her.

To her, to her, to her, for her, for her, for her — why couldn't I tear my eyes out so I could not see her things?

Why couldn't I drive the words out? *For her, for her.*

Blast my eardrums with fourteen speakers on high volume. Rock 'n' roll is here to stay. I turned all the music on high to let it fill me from the inside out, to take up all the empty space. Maybe I could be emptied into a bag with a skin on the outside and rock 'n' roll on the inside. The louder the better. So loud that I couldn't hear a thing at all.

Nothing made the pain go away.

■ ■ ■

I went to the vegetable patch Alex had put in. Gabrielle's rabbits were out back, out of the bunny stage and on their way to being rabbits. The door was latched shut, but the key was on a string tied to the chicken wire. The lock opened easily.

"Move. Move."

I flushed the bunnies out of the pen. It was three feet off the ground, but they could make the jump. Some landed hard, bumping their noses on the soft dirt when they came out of the cage crooked, but they hopped off toward the high grass, first with small steps, then with bounds.

"Get out, you."

One little bunny was hunched in the back of the cage, afraid to move. It was black with bright, shiny eyes. I reached my hand into the cage to grab it and release it. But when my hand closed around its neck, I squeezed. Squeezed it harder and harder. Its throat inside my hand. There was a little pop. One of its eyes was red with blood collected inside it. The other was only a mirror. I could see myself in the eye. It was no longer a creature seeing me but only a mirror reflecting me.

I knew it was still alive. Its back legs were kicking but its front legs were paralyzed. I put it in a shoe box and closed the lid on it. I put a rubber band around the box. Then I got in the truck and threw it off the New River bridge.

The box turning end over end in its fall.

The little, black bunny falling and falling.

Hitting rock.

And what is the purpose of the groundhog to the Creation?

 Marianne didn't want Ralph at the house. To her, I was the guy with AIDS. I wasn't Zack Rosen, the man who made the bike. I wasn't Zack Rosen who provided the turkey on Thanksgiving. I wasn't the man who owned a hundred-year-old house, a stream, and the water rights. Or the converted Jew who sat in the white-pine pew of Johnny's church. Or the man who had just lost his wife and stepdaughter. I was *that man with AIDS*.

But I didn't have AIDS. I had HIV. Human immunodeficiency virus. The name must have been invented by someone who thought it was important to state that humans got it. In the beginning, it was named this to separate the virus from ape — simian — immune deficiency syndrome. Some people think it got started from Africans fucking monkeys. I met a guy named Randall, a Vietnam vet who studied acupressure and Korean herbs, who told me it came from the steroids given to beef. In the digestion process, the disease starts in the intestine. "Death begins in the colon" was his favorite expression. Who knows, maybe it was the government hepatitis trials that caused it — that virus was so wicked, it could not come from nature. Maybe even the name had a double meaning: "human" because humans got it, "human" because humans made it.

Marianne didn't want Ralph to come over. But he came anyway.

"I come to put in the Jacuzzi," he knocked at the door the first time since Shelley died. He carried his toolbox. Even though it was early spring, he wore a down vest over his work shirt. His work truck was parked down the driveway, out on the shoulder of the road.

"Sure, Ralph. You know where the bedroom is."

Normally, I would have gone upstairs and talked to him while he worked. But I didn't. I went back to the sofa with all the shades pulled down. I had headaches day and night, and I laid there with a wet cloth over my eyes. It was night-dark in the room. I didn't want to see anything, see anybody. In the dark, noises sound louder, cold strikes more to the bone.

"You all right, buddy?" Ralph asked, pulling off his sunglasses.

"Yeah," I said without moving.

"That was a stupid question. What I mean is, you can't just lie here till you die, Zack."

"Yeah, right," I thought. Why not?

I said to Ralph the one thing I had been afraid even to think before. It was so horrible that I could not live with that thought one second in my mind. But since he was here, since he been touched by the Lord, and since he was such a good friend, I said what was on my heart.

"She knew what she was doing, Ralph. She infected me. She did it on purpose."

"She knew she was infected?"

"She did it on purpose."

"No."

Ralph dropped into the chair by the sofa. A long sigh broke the air.

"I remember with the twins," he said.

"She changed the life insurance policy. That's only one thing."

"She knew."

He started to make that ironic howling laugh at ourselves. We used to get so much fun out of it, howling at ourselves from a margin of safety. Because even though we were assholes about how our lives got fucked up, the fuckups only screwed us in small ways. Money lost could be gotten back. Marianne was a bitch, but Ralph was going to leave her. Sure, every now and then, she got hairy and left the house with a shotgun and sleeping pills, so the kids would call Ralph, but nothing ever came of it except that Ralph rushed over there to find Marianne sitting smug on the sofa with her arms folded across her chest. So Ralph was an asshole in that department. I had been an asshole in the same department, the department of pussy-whipped, but it wasn't so bad because it gave us a place to belong. Even though the price for that belonging was high, those women keeping us on a tight line, pulling up on the choker chain now and then to let us know who was boss, it was only that. We could laugh at that. But now it all turned in a different direction, that what we thought was innocent was not innocent, that the choker chain had a razor edge on it.

Nothing came out of Ralph's howling mouth. He repeated, "The twins that returned from the grave."

"She didn't even tell me. Three years we was married. She could have told me. I would have married her even if she was infected. I supported her. I took care of her children. Everything."

"You could have used a *condom.*"

We were only two voices talking in the dark. I couldn't see his face. Maybe I was too ashamed that my wife had done that to me. There was the pain. The shame. Why should I be ashamed for getting a death sentence? I was such a fool.

"She had it all worked out. She had flex time. She didn't cook or clean. I was never home. She never told anyone at work. She kept it all to herself. And then, she just died. She didn't have to die. If they knew it was pneumonia, they could have given her some antibiotics or something. She hid it from everyone. I think Gabrielle knew. She must have known something."

"Yeah, but if Shelley told you, then you would know, wouldn't you? The doctor would know. Someone woulda known. No one knew."

Ralph didn't work on the Jacuzzi that day. We sat in the dark, turned on some records, played the Moody Blues at full volume in the dark.

 I put an ad in the newspaper to sell my house and all my furniture. I thought I was going to die immediately. Most of my good furniture went, no big surprise since I sold it for a song. After I sold my kitchen dinette set, my good coffee table and cabinets, I woke up one morning without anything to eat on. I thought I was going to die. But I didn't. And I had no functional furniture.

The day Ralph brought over the pizza and the dinette set, he had a woman with him. A younger woman. "This is my boss at work," he said. He dropped the pizza in a rubbery cardboard box into the center of the living room floor. "Get up, Zack," he said. I did even though I didn't want to. The three of us sat around the pizza in the dark like we were Indians around a campfire. In the dark Ralph reached under the pizza box and squeezed Patrice's hand.

"He made the Harley," Ralph said. "I wanted to show Patrice who made the Harley."

"It's a beautiful bike," she said.

"It's Ralph's now," I said. The pizza did not go down too easily.

"What do you say, Zack? I got a dinette set in the back of the truck."

"What are you doing with a dinette set?"

"We were doing some work on a house," Patrice said. She had a low, raspy voice that sounded like sawing. I could see why Ralph liked her. She spoke softly. "They left it in the house."

"I sold my dinette set," I said.

"So, you gonna eat on the floor the rest of your life?"

"Ralph, I could go any minute."

"I don't think so, buddy. I think you'll make it to your next meal. Which means you need a dinette set."

"I can't give you anything for it, Ralph," I said.

"Maybe you'll let me eat on it sometime."

"Any time you want."

"He's been living in his truck," Patrice said, getting up and walking outside, the door slamming shut behind her as if she was mad.

"All the time you been working on the bathroom, you been living in your truck?"

"It's all right."

"I got four bedrooms, Ralph. The house is empty."

"You got enough on your plate all ready, buddy."

"My plate, your plate, what's that got to do with anything? I can't eat on no table alone, Ralph."

"We'll talk about it later," he said, as Patrice came through the front door carrying one of the chairs, Ralph pointing down the corridor to the kitchen.

"It's got four chairs," Ralph said.

"Is she going to ruin your testimony?" I asked him.

"I'm all right with the Lord," he said.

At the morning service at Johnny's cinder-block church in Montvale, Johnny called me to the front. He put his arm around my shoulder, hugging me up in front of the congregation. He hugged me so tightly, my shoulders bunched up together.

"This man is afflicted with the HIV. I have known him since he moved here. I will stand by him. Even if it is me and him against the world, I will stand by him. I will find a mighty oak, the oak which is the Lord, and I will put my back against the oak and be strong against the world to anyone who turns away from this innocent man, Zachariah Rosen, who did nothing evil but love his wife. As the Bible says we are to love."

Everyone came up to me after the service, hugging me, and saying they were so sorry. All crying.

■ ■ ■

Three boys in Florida lived together in the same house. Someone burned down the house and killed them because they had AIDS.

I spent a lot of time thinking, my mind on high idle. *Hummida hummida hummida.* My wife betrayed me. She lied to me. Lied to me about the number of marriages she had. Lied to me about the number of children she had. Lied to me about everything. And she gave me a disease.

I was always full of life. I loved life. Now it was to be taken away from me. I tried to understand the Lord's ways. I wasn't always a good person, but I always knew that God was close. Even when I did stupid things, I was close to the Lord.

Could that virus be of God? It's hard to imagine that nature made such a bug, and yet, it says in Scripture that the rain falls on the just and the unjust. If Jesus went walking through the rain, you think He'd stay dry because He was of God? No. He would get wet. That's what that Scripture means. If that virus gets in your bloodstream, you get the virus. It doesn't know the difference between sinner and saint. It is just like the rain, making no discrimination. Nature doesn't make discriminations. But then, God does.

■ ■ ■

The rain fell steadily all spring. The grass in the back sprouted up. The creek filled up so high, the water came to the middle of the drainpipe under the road, and that pipe was ten feet in diameter. Up the mountain, the snows from a hard winter were melting. The drainpipes from my sinks and tub ran out through a pipe in the yard, and the end of the pipe opened on the stream. Usually, the place over the pipe would be green with the ground soft around it. This spring, all the ground, ten, fifteen feet on either side of the pipe, was soft and mushy. The house practically floated on its foundation. The pussy willows were popping out on the branches and were getting ready to bloom. The water rose so high, I worried about the willow tree tilting into the creek. Every so often, I said to Ralph, "We're going to lose that tree, Ralph."

He shook his head, meaning maybe yes, maybe no, it was all in the Lord's hands.

Water was everywhere. Everything — green, green, green. You looked up, you'd see little leaves on all the branches, high and low, in the tallest tree to the shortest shrub. Look down and there'd be grass growing so fast, a foot wouldn't leave an imprint. All around in the yard, flimsy weeds grew woody stalks. The ladybugs came thick and fast, hatching inside the house, covering the ceiling. You sat down, there was a ladybug crawling up your butthole. You opened your mouth to breathe, six flew up your nostrils. It was spring, with life going a hundred miles an hour like a pestilence, only this was a pestilence of life.

My driving mower sat with a full tank of gas in the shed.

Me and the Lord having a chat. That's what Jews do by being Jewish. Talk to God.

Me: I got HIV. My wife betrayed me. I lost my stepdaughter (even though she was mean to me). I lost my job. I got no income. I went bankrupt. Can you tell me why, Lord?

Lord: It's raining outside.

Me: I got this disease. But you can do anything. You healed Ralph of his cancer. You raised the dead. You raised Lazarus. I don't understand. But I believe you got a plan for me. I believe there is a purpose to this. Can you tell me what the purpose is?

But the Lord did not disclose His purpose to me. Why should He? He is the Lord. When I turn on the Discovery station, I watched the shows about the beginning of the universe, shows with all the planets, stars, and asteroids. I look outside, and I see Shelley's roses growing up the trellis. The grass keeps growing, and I mean nothing to it. My spiritual nature looks at the world and says, *Do you really think the God who made this is going to answer you back? Don't you have any respect for this?*

(Was this the purpose? To teach me respect?)

I never respected authority. My mother beat me with the wooden spoon, my old man left the house. I was the outlaw, the kid walking out of class, the maverick in the black leather jacket and the boots laying down rubber in the parking lot outside the principal's office. The one who slipped through the cracks.

I was the kid who at seventeen traded cars, buying and selling them like they were baseball cards. Once they were mine, they were *mine,* and I did anything I wanted with them.

Like the Chevy I used to own. It broke down. Frankie, then a boy, looked at it, him and me watching the car in the yard as the snow fell. I said, "Let's fill this car up with snow." We took shovels to fill up the inside of the car. We packed the interior of the car full of it. The body was black. In the spring, the snow melted, and the car was ruined. Did this show respect, I ask you, for the car? Someone made it. I paid for it. It was my car. I could do what I want with it, couldn't I? Or was this disrespect for a made thing, a functional thing on earth, that, even though it was mine, had its way of existing in the world?

I always treated my body good. I trained it up. Ate right. Never smoked. Never drank. I respected my body as a temple of the Holy Spirit. Was I supposed to learn respect? I didn't always have respect on the small scale, but in the big picture I did, so why would I need to learn it?

Maybe this affliction was not about me — teaching me this

or that — but about God, God wanting to show His glory, God pushing me right to the edge so I could be healed. That's what Ralph thinks: God has a plan for me.

I was always marked by God, everyone could see that.

In the Book of Job, the Lord says, "Where was thou when I laid the foundations of the earth?" and "Shall he that contendeth with the Almighty instruct him? He that reproveth God, let him answer it."

Job knew he was in trouble. After the Lord spoke, Job said, "Behold I am vile; what shall I answer thee? I will clap my hand over my mouth. Once have I spoken; but I will not answer."

I'd go through spells when I couldn't eat. My weight went up and down. I dropped thirty pounds from not eating after Shelley died. I lay in the dark wondering why.

Ralph says, "The Lord chose you for this. When He heals you of this affliction, you will really show His glory."

Ralph just had cancer. It was a relatively minor glory. AIDS is the big one. The 23rd Psalm says, "Yea, though I walk *through* the valley of the shadow of death, I will fear no evil."

No double messages here. Scripture was straight on the money about the healing power of God. Walk *through*.

Some people are healed through death.

If the rain falls on the just and the unjust, can there be a purpose in the righteous getting wet? And so, if it was just an accident that I got infected and not any kind of moral act, then I should just accept it as an act of nature. But if God has a purpose for everything, then how could this be an innocent act? He supports the lilies of the field and puts the air under the wings of hawks. If God takes so much interest in all the creatures of nature, and I am a creature of nature, God must have an interest in me, and so there must be a purpose.

I thought God wanted me to marry Shelley. He guided me to her.

When I began to speak in churches I thought my purpose was to teach the will of God through my testimony. It started with Johnny letting me preach in his church. Eventually I began to speak in churches and religion classes. The pastors didn't let gay people in to speak to the youth groups, but I was a heterosexual. Maybe some good was done in that some young people avoided death, even though some pastors forbade me to talk about condoms.

 The next time Ralph came over with Patrice was to put in the bathroom upstairs. He brought a Jacuzzi tub from B&B as part of our trade in the bike deal. When he came into the house, he turned on the light in the dining room.

"My God," he said. "What have you been doing, Zack?"

"I been painting my house," I said.

I bought paint with the money I got from Shelley's life insurance. When I went to the paint store, I looked for something bright. Whatever color I saw, I bought enough paint to paint the room. I painted the dining room blue.

When Ralph finished putting in the Jacuzzi in the bathroom upstairs, I bought purple paint. I like purple, no matter where it is: in flowers, on cars, upholstery, walls. After Ralph mirrored the wall above the Jacuzzi, I painted the bare walls purple. Shelley had a statue of a woman bending over a water pot, almost a lifesize statue, so I put her in one corner of the Jacuzzi.

When you sat on the john, you could look across at the Jacuzzi and see the woman bent over the side like she was drawing water from the well. If you looked down, you could see your naked hairy legs, dropped jeans, and boots in the mirror.

Ralph had a good laugh on me for the color. "It's so much, Zack."

I asked him if he was going to move in with me. He asked if I would paint his room.

"If you want," I told him. "I'll paint it any color you want, buddy. It's all yours."

The two of us walked through the house just in case he wanted to pick one of the rooms. The upstairs room where the daughter of Satan had lived was now white, but that red carpet remained. Even though we never had a dog, it smelled like wet dog. That room should have been a happier place as it had windows on two of the walls.

The downstairs room, the Harley room, had junk in it, but it was biker junk. Harley parts. Shelley's books. The chest of drawers. The white room was still a junk room, with my free weights and weight belt in it.

Ralph liked the Harley room. He could go in and out and bypass the rest of the house. Privacy was important for him. I could understand it.

"I can't believe you did all this painting in the house, Zack," he said.

"Come back to the shed with me, Ralph. I got something else to show you."

"Have you been working on the truck?"

"I been to Sears. I bought a weed eater."

"You need one," he said. "The weeds in the ditch are looking ugly."

"Two hundred dollars. I bought the Deluxe."

It was time to take my mower out.

When I decided to live, I bought a weed eater.

 When Ralph comes in the door, he's tired from working on the house. Patrice is on the rag and has been on his case at work. He brings in a two-dollar pizza from Kroger and puts it in the microwave. Marianne won't sign the divorce paper. He's behind on the rent. We're both low on our money — me because I am disabled and Ralph because he's paying support for his children. Too, he's still paying on the half mountain he used to own and the tractor and the cattle that's on it, so he's always broke. As we watch the tank, eating pizza off napkins, Ralph jokes about the fish.

"Maybe we should take one of those little ones out, Zack," he says meaning that we are broke enough to eat our own fish.

"They're eating each other. They don't need us to eat them."

"So what did you do today, buddy?"

"I found a convent, Ralph. They gave me some lunch. I told them my story."

"What did you have?"

"Never mind the food. You should have seen the nun. She was pretty. Why would a pretty woman be a nun? Do you think she hates men?"

"Maybe she just loves the Lord."

"She was so beautiful."

With a face like an angel, pure white skin, and little hands. You could see the blue veins beneath the skin. She had hands like my fish, see-through.

 I was born good. God made me good. But the truth is this — though I have long since made my peace with my mother and nobody likes to talk about it, especially us men — I grew up a beaten boy. Nowadays people will speak about abuse. I was abused. Mabel beat me. Later, when I was in my thirties and she needed a by-pass surgery, I talked to her. I said, "You didn't treat me very good, Mom." She told me, "You were the first. You don't know what to do with the first one. Live and learn."

So it was that, an accident of birth. Live and learn. Well, it was practice for her, but it was my flesh that hurt, my heart that got broken. Maybe I kept looking for older women to mend the rift with my mother. Frieda was practically a mother to me. But with Shelley, it was different, because she was a Leviticus Jew. She was my kind. My tribe.

Why would she do this to me?

No one talks much about women abusing men.

I hit her once. I know a man must never touch a woman. I was brought up right in that respect. But how can I explain the extreme circumstances that drove me to that?

I can tell you this: I have had this disease for three years already, and I don't know what I would do if I couldn't talk about it. But there she was, dying and knowing it, and she couldn't talk about it. She must have been going crazy inside her mind.

But why would she want to kill me?

Lord, did you hear me? Why would she want to kill me?

■ ■ ■

"He will make a way where there is no way," comes off the CD with gospel music. I have CDS now instead of records. One day I woke up and felt I had to do *something*. I believed that my records were of the devil. I called up Johnny and asked him if he would help me. Ralph brought over his pickup truck from work. We parked it close to the house with the rear end angled at the steps, the tailgate open. We took hours to load the truck with my records, and then we drove it to the church where the deacons already piled up wood for a bonfire. It was the middle of winter, so that fire felt good. Ralph and I climbed in the back of the truck and handed the records down to whoever was around, maybe eight or ten men from church, and they carried them to the fire to burn them. I must have burned up $10,000 worth of records.

"That's the end of them," I told Johnny and Ralph.

Ralph said, "Watch out, Zack. The wind is changing."

The smoke came out of the fire in a blue-black cloud like an oil slick. The wind changed, and Johnny started coughing so he covered his face with a handkerchief. The smoke blew over to the house across the street. "They're devil worshipers," one deacon said. The smoke covered the side of the house like a tornado with the tail of it coming out of the fire.

Everyone was all right with smoking out the worshipers of Satan.

Something told me I had to burn those records. Later I knew it wasn't the music that was bad. It was just something I had to do.

Now I'm replacing them all with CDs.

The Lord has sent me many afflictions of the body. Diarrhea. Nausea. Chronic fatigue. The afflictions were doubled by the therapies for them. It was hard on Ralph. He was with me all the way, but he remembered me when I was huge, with arms as big around as pipes and handsome enough that hookers would give me goody for nothing if I'd have wanted it. He couldn't stand to see me lose weight, going down, down, down, down; that was why he brought the pot plants into the house to begin with. We'd smoke dope together, then he'd go down to a pizza place that had real New York pizza and bring me something I could eat. I didn't really like smoking that much, but it gave me an appetite. Then I realized it was ruining my testimony. Eventually Dr. Phillips prescribed Maranol for me, which is the legal government version of pot, but that drug made me so high, it took the life out of me. I'd take it, get a buzz, and then couldn't get up out of the bed for days, so I quit taking it.

After I joined the HIV support group, I began to get invitations to speak in schools and churches about the disease. They wanted me because I am not gay or an intravenous drug user. That stuff ultimately doesn't make any difference. You got the disease and that's it. The gay guys used to kid me a lot when I went on retreats, saying they were ready for me if I wanted to cross over. It was all friendly.

I know what the Bible says about homosexuality in the book named for my tribe, the book of Leviticus. A man should not lie down with a man or with an animal. I never was interested in men. Here I was a two hundred–pound trucker, a Messianic Jew with the same disease as gay men, and people looked at me like I was gay. But the young people loved me. I would go to talk in the western Virginia schools, and the administrators said, "Don't say anything about condoms."

You look at all those kids, teenagers — young girls looking at me like it was all a fairy tale and maybe they could take me home and heal me up with their love, or maybe they had someone in their lives they could heal with love — me knowing that I was one of the few speakers the school administrators even let in to talk to these kids, yet I couldn't talk about condoms.

What if those kids were already *doing* it?

My testimony was three-fold: my heritage, my affliction, and my salvation. For heritage, I was a Leviticus Jew come to Christ. My affliction was my disease, and my salvation was my faith. I didn't hate anyone. I didn't hate Shelley. I forgave her. I loved her. Love was of me, and it was good. Maybe she didn't treat me well, but that didn't take away my love for her. I went around to churches and gave my testimony. Sometimes the congregation would make a special collection to give me a love offering, which I really needed because I lived on disability.

Life wasn't so bad. In the summer, Ralph and I sat out on the porch. Ralph has an eagle eye and can spot the double star in the Big Dipper. We'd sit out there and watch the stars, him telling me about the things that I could not see.

"I hope I live long enough to die here," I tell him.

He cracks up.

My brothers disowned me. They didn't want to admit that someone in their family had AIDS.

Some people say that this disease is God's punishment on the wicked. I have been to a lot of hospitals and nursing homes. I've seen infants with cancer, with tumors, with AIDS.

So, what are they being punished for?

Johnny let me preach in his church whenever I felt the call. He even let me take over his morning radio show twice. It was a call-in show. During the show, I gave out my personal phone number. When I was interviewed on Christian television for an hour, my telephone number was given out, and the show ran three times that week. But the only people who ever called me at home were either infected or crazy. One girl called and asked me to visit her brother in the hospital. He had gone in with pneumonia, and they discovered he was infected then. He had been infected a couple of years and didn't know it until he came in for something else.

Another guy called me. He was thirty-eight, the son of a minister, and he tested positive. He estimated that he was infected for eight years. All that time, he never suspected. He practiced unprotected sex. A minister's son who lived at home.

My phone registers the numbers of the people who call me. I got a call from "Out of Area." His name was Bobby. He said, "Zack, I heard you on the radio. I got to get help. Before I do it again. I know you'll understand. Them little boys . . ."

I couldn't call the police because I didn't have his number. I said, "Bobby, anytime you think about doing something, call me first. Or talk to your minister. Talk to someone."

Bobby calls me every month or so. Just to see how I am. Says he thinks about me. That's all. Wonders how I am.

A reporter named Cody from the city paper called me. He wanted to do an interview for the religion column. He came over, took my picture, and interviewed me about having the disease.

I knew I was doing the Lord's work.

This was the purpose.

God had given me this affliction, and I would spread His Word through it. Once I had been lost — my life empty and chaotic — now my life was full with my understanding. I had been hungry for my destiny; now, I lived it.

But the people who called me on the phone or who came to my house were not like me. They were more like Bobby.

After Cody's article on me appeared on the front page of the newspaper, a Jewish woman called me. She had a niece, an Israeli woman who was a Christian. The niece was very shy, but perhaps I could help her. She also had a weight problem. I seemed so sure of myself in the paper, the aunt said, maybe I could help the niece, who was twenty-three and had a problem with self-esteem. I met the niece and her uncle at a coffee shop. The niece wore army boots laced up to below her knees. She wore green army pants. She was huge. Her butt, literally, was so big, she needed two chairs for it. But instead, she sat in one seat, and the rest hung over. She also had a mustache. I explained my story to them, said they should trust the Lord, and that I had to go to give another talk.

One girl from Virginia Tech called me to do an interview. I met her at the coffee place downtown. She had short brown hair and a red mouth. She wore baggy black jeans two sizes too big and walked like she had heavy feet. She asked me some questions, like did I date or go out with anyone. I said I didn't. As we were leaving she offered to give me a ride to my truck. I said all right. I was feeling tired, doing a lot of driving in and out of town to the same coffee shop to meet people about speaking engagements.

The girl said, "If you want to screw me, we can do it on the backseat." She had condoms. She said, "You're so exciting, I'm creaming the seat right now."

They crawled out of the woodwork. Women who liked that black-leather biker look, liked to live on the edge of danger, thinking there was something sexy in being close to death. I still had my health then. I thought that girl must be out of her mind if she wanted to fool around with something like this. I did not want to ruin my testimony. My life had to stand behind the work I was doing for God.

I jumped out of that girl's car at the first red light.

I jumped and ran down the road. Running and running, like I couldn't go far enough fast enough to get away. I wanted to get away from it all. From the disease. From the crazy people who came to me. While some people avoided me because I had the disease, other people wanted to be around me *because* I had the disease. Like Bobby, him thinking a man with HIV and a child molester had something in common.

I was so much on the outside of normal life, other outsiders identified with me. They thought we had something in common. People would tell me, "Zack, I want you to meet someone," and bring over a woman with three children. The woman didn't work. She'd be in the house with screaming kids, looking around at my yard, my furniture, and I knew what she was thinking: "If I use a condom, it will be all right. And my kids will have the house." Some people thought that I would be so desperate, I would be grateful for anyone to love me. That's what the Israeli uncle with his niece believed. I was an attractive Jewish man with a house, and maybe my AIDS balanced his niece's fat ass. Or maybe I would want her *because* I had AIDS. After all, only a desperate woman would want a man with AIDS.

Maybe that's why Shelley never told me. What kind of man would want a woman with AIDS? With a daughter? Who can love the hated of the earth? The most reviled? Mothers pull their children out from under my eyes when they recognize me. Preachers pull their hand away from mine. Grown men and women watch the place my hand, my mouth, my foot has been long after it's gone. You know they're thinking, "What did he leave behind?" Aloneness, it's the worst.

Bobby the child molester calls me more often than my brother.

And what if even Bobby did not call me?

 I thought no one would ever love me again because I was infected. Then I realized you can't compromise love.

I realized this because a year after Shelley died, I met a public health worker. When I was in her office, applying for social services, she invited me to tea. She was an attractive woman, a brunette, a little older than me. She wore dresses with hose like Shelley.

Later she told me, "I have to have you." She had never married before even though she had a twelve-year-old daughter, like Shelley. She could never find the man of her dreams, she said, until she met me. So we got married. She moved into my house with her daughter. Ralph had moved in with me by that time and, like Shelley, Jennifer was always on my ass about kicking him out. But Ralph was divorcing Marianne, and he had no place else to go. He wasn't paying me rent. No way I could kick him out of my house. After a while, it was real clear that Jennifer and I both had made a mistake, not calculating correctly what we were getting into. So we divorced.

Ralph said he thought that she thought I was going to die immediately and that she would get the house. But then I didn't die on the spot. That taught me you can't compromise love. I married her because I was desperate and afraid, but it was wrong, and that's all I have to say about my third wife except that there was a third. We were married less than a year. I had two wives I divorced and one I remained with till death.

Me, by Jewish tradition and Christian faith, supposed to stay with a woman for life. Ralph saying he felt sorry for Jennifer, she didn't have a chance in my heart against Shelley's memory.

When I fill out medical forms, I don't know which box to check for marital status. I was all of the above: single, divorced, and widowed. I don't want to talk anymore about Jennifer. Sometimes I'll see her in town, and she'll look away. When my newspaper article came out, she called me up. I didn't answer the phone though because, as I have said, I don't answer the phone anymore.

 This idea had the hand of God in it. It came out of the blue even though at the same time it seemed like an idea that had been there all along. Because this idea was instant but always there, I knew it was of God. You just know things like this: you wake up one morning with the full realization of your purpose on earth.

I knew that I would not die until I gave my testimony in the New Valley Baptist Church. It was revealed to me.

Meanwhile, Marianne told everyone in Johnny's church that I had ruined her marriage because I let Ralph stay at my house. Marianne went to New Valley after she had the fight with Johnny about the "chatter of women."

Marianne hated me so much — she made a special clause in her divorce papers that proved it. Ralph showed me.

He said, "Zack. Look at this."

He was standing in the kitchen eating a bagel over the sink. He was losing weight too, like we were sympathetic, but he was still working on the house at the lake. He'd put in forty hours a week making cabinets, and then he and Patrice left work to make a $300,000 house together. It went up a nail at a time.

"I can't believe it," Ralph said. Then he laughed and howled, which he did when he was nervous.

His contract of divorce had a special clause in it. None of his children could visit him at his current residence as long as he lived with a man with AIDS.

"She's just doing this to hurt you, Ralph," I said, folding the papers up and handing them back to him. "She's using me to hurt you."

"She had her attorney put it in. I can't believe it."

He squinted his eyes and shook his head back and forth. I know it hurt him that she would do that. I like women but this Marianne was a cold, anus-mouthed woman. No one knew for sure about Ralph and Patrice in public, but Marianne suspected.

To cheer ourselves up, Ralph and I decided to go to the Kroger to get some ice cream for supper. It was cold outside, dusk coming on but not yet arrived. We went on the bike, my Harley/his Harley/*the* Harley. Even with leathers, the cold air cut through to the bone. Ralph laughed in the wind, I could feel him. Riding along on the bike, for once I felt free again, the road unwinding in front of us without lights or signs on the way. Not even streetlights. For a few minutes, going fast on the highway, I got to feel the whole thing: freedom and forgetfulness tied up in a ball.

In front of the dairy case in Kroger, I said, "Ralph, look at us."

We were reflected in the case. Two bikers from Jersey with sunglasses and leathers. Ralph's hair fell below his shoulders; he had trimmed up his beard and mustache. My beard covered half my chest. Woolly beard. Woolly hair. Moses Unchained.

Two tough Jersey bikers reflected over Breyer's vanilla bean.

Ralph gave a small howling laugh as he picked out the Heavenly Hash. I got coffee ice cream because I didn't drink coffee anymore.

Two pussy-whipped motherfuckers in leathers buying ice cream to take the sting out of life.

Then neither of us had enough money straight out to pay for it. First he dug through his jacket pockets, then his pants pockets for change. I gave him some change but ended up writing a check. For three dollars of ice cream.

Woodstock survivors.

 "It will be like going to sleep," I told Frankie, my younger brother, over the phone. I started seeing a therapist who helped me work out coping skills. I asked her all the time about the end. If I were lucky, if I didn't get too many opportunistic infections, I would go to sleep one day and not wake up. Dr. Phillips also gave me a prescription for Valium and sleeping pills. Most of the people in my support group were heavy into mood pills. With AIDS, it takes a long, long time to die. In 80 percent of cases, the mind goes, but not until the end. The rest of the time, you know you got it. You know where it ends. You know what everyone thinks about you. They think: you might as well be in the grave already. Sometimes I hear people say, "If I knew I had AIDS, I would shoot myself in the head." They act like if you had any brains, you would kill yourself. Why wait around and suffer?

But nobody wants to die. The body wants to live. The spirit wants to live. Your heart still wants the same things as other people: love, respect. You still want to laugh. You still want to ride Harleys and feel spring come. To drive a truck again, bring in a check again, be a good provider. Touch a woman's hair without her drawing back, kiss her deep in the mouth without her gagging. Run or pump iron, eat ice cream without getting the shits. Stay awake. Stay awake through your life instead of sleeping through the main points. How do you keep being a man when you can do none of the things a man's supposed to do? Yet you know you are a man.

It's only other people who want you to die.

Some days I don't even know I have it.

Some days I do.

■ ■ ■

Frankie called me a week or so before I picked up the phone directly. Because the machine said "Out of Area," I thought it might have been Bobby. He called me to ask me did I put my affairs in order.

Son of a bitch.

When Ralph came home early from working on the house, we sat on the porch together.

Watching the traffic drive by the house was just like looking at water in the tank or fish swimming in the aquarium. It was soothing. You could see the headlights come around the bend on the southern side, then tip down as the car went through the valley. They came around and down the hill with a flicker of lights.

"What'd you do today, buddy?" Ralph asked me.

"Nothing much."

"Everything is nothing much."

"Come on."

"You come on."

Two or so years after I took myself off AZT, I saw the new Harley. It was a 1986 Harley, made before I was infected. Gray with black points. The asking price was only $10,000. If I could cash in my life insurance policy, I could buy it. From the insurance point of view, I am dead on paper. I have $29,000 in death benefits on my life insurance. A special company, organized for persons with AIDS, promises me a 60 to 80 percent return on my benefits. All I have to do is fill in the paperwork.

"They want a list of your medications," Ralph says.

He is helping me fill out forms so I can collect my death benefits before I die.

Eight bottles of pills and tablets, two creams, some lozenges are lined up on the kitchen table.

"There's not enough room on this form," he says, starting to fill in the blank. "But," he adds, "I'll write a note and say 'continued on back.'"

I hand him one phial after another so he can take the name off the bottle.

"I found a bike, Ralph."

"Yeah, what year?"

"Nineteen eighty-six. Same model as yours. You should see it, Ralph," I tell him. "He wants $10,000. It's really worth much more. In New York, you could sell it for twice that much."

"Opportunistic infections. How many you had? Thrush?"

"Yes."

"Pneumonia."

"No. Thank the Lord. The Bactrim is for that, Ralph. It's prophylactic against pneumonia. It's the only bike in his showroom."

"CMV?"

"No."

"What the hell is it?"

"It causes blindness."

"What's the one cats give you?"

"Toxoplasmosis."

"'No' on that, right?"

"Right."

"I got to take a break."

Ralph goes outside to smoke on the porch. I don't allow him to smoke in the house any place except his bedroom and the outside. Cigarette smoke irritates my lungs. I see him walk circles on the porch. He blows the smoke out of his lungs so that it sounds like a deep sigh. Even from the kitchen, I can hear the porch groan under his feet. Car lights speeding down the road flicker over him like a strobe. Then he lights another cigarette. In his walking circles, he walks in and out of his own smoke.

I made a bike from parts once. Now I can buy one already built. A new Harley. It felt like being in love all over again.

When Ralph comes back in the house, he says, "I'm sorry. I can't finish this for you. Anyhow, you won't have to pay it back after you're healed."

Ralph and I share the Word. It feels like we have a secret between us. The Lord healed him of class-five melanoma skin cancer. He has seen death, he knows what it feels like, so he gives me hope. When we christianize, we are sometimes happy, or maybe at rest, with this secret. Ralph says, "Trust in the Lord. He will make a way where there is no way. You know the meaning of lukewarm?"

We were sitting on the porch swing one evening when I could still drive. Two blue bowls of ice cream with chocolate pooled in the bottom rested on the floor. The stars were bright in the cool air, the sky was moonless, and only the screech of tires interrupted the crickets.

"It means not too hot or too cold."

"Do you know what's wrong with lukewarm?" Ralph continues.

"Tell me, Ralph."

"It means you got no conviction. Hot and cold, those are extremes. 'Extremes' mean you go all the way to the end. No matter what your view, you take it to the end, to the extreme. 'Lukewarm' means you stay in the middle. You don't take a side."

"The in-betweens," I say, "it's hard living in the in-betweens."

"The Lord blesses the extremes. You are taking it all the way, Zack. The Lord blessed you. He gave you a vehicle to show His glory. When you are healed, everyone will know the glory of the Lord."

At the very thought of it, Ralph laughs. "All of those people, everyone who says there is no cure, they will sure be surprised. When the Lord heals you, everyone will know."

"All the time, I'm waiting. The Lord knows I wait for Him, Ralph."

"He knows, Zack. Remember: 'He will make a way where there is no way.'"

"Praise the Lord, Ralph. But Ralph . . ."

"Yeah, Zack."

"I wish you'd quit smoking."

He says, "He will make a way."

 After Jennifer, wife number three, left, I started buying the paper more often. I searched the paper every day looking for a cure. I looked in the big print, in the small print. I got connected up with the local AIDS coalition, and the director told me about a priest who was started a healing ministry; he wanted to work specifically with persons with AIDS. This appealed to me because everything I encountered was just the opposite, that most churches did not want to work with anyone with AIDS. This priest worked out of a place called the Healing Light Center; he told me to come out. I went there December 6, 1993. It was the feast day of their saint, St. Nicholas.

The priest was over sixty years old and balder than my father. He learned about healing when he was in a war in Guatemala. Far out in the country, in the villages, young children were getting shot up by rebel troops. One day a young boy got shot and went into a coma. His mother came for this priest, Father Dan, who looked down at him. The boy's face was losing its color, blood was on the edge of his mouth, dirt and blood coated his cheeks. The priest said that at that moment he knew it was only God and him. No ambulance, no paramedics, no 911 in the middle of a war. So he prayed. He felt an energy pass through him, coming from God and going into his arms and out his hands. It went into the boy. Whose eyes blinked, whose breathing leveled out, whose mother carried her son home across her back, joyful.

I went there, to the Healing Light Center. After a Mass, people collected in a meeting room, some ten or twelve of us with the priest at the front of the room.

Father Dan said that people who came there to be healed wanted to learn how to heal; he was hoping to staff his ministry with those converts. There was a fiftyish woman with strawlike hair and thin shoulders who came with her son, a bullet-headed young man who wore hiking boots, a gay guy with a thin nose, fat hips, and an earring. His name was Pedro. The forty-something woman there was a Jew, I could tell by instinct. Her hair was frizzed out like a poodle. She called herself Judith. She hated me on sight, I could feel it. There was also a little woman, thirties or forties, with brown hair and tight pants, who smiled at me when I came so I took a seat next to her. She had talked to me before Mass. At the beginning of the meeting, we held hands to pray, and I held her hand a little longer at the end.

When I got home, I told Ralph: "I met a woman. At church."

He clapped his hand to his forehead and said, "Zack, what are you telling me? You met a woman at *church*? Have I heard this before?"

"She's my age."

"How many children does she have?"

"You won't believe this. None."

He laughed and laughed. "That's what they all say."

That little woman was my age, forty, and had never been married. I kept asking her over and over if she had any children. She said no. I kept asking. She knew I was infected because I told her. She held my hand in church during the prayers. I didn't let her hand go. She kept saying, "I really don't have any children."

 In order to fulfill what I believe was the Lord's purpose for me — giving my testimony at New Valley Baptist Church — I made an appointment and went to the deacon, Mike Viola. I asked could I give my testimony. He said I wasn't a preacher and couldn't go behind the pulpit. I said, "The Lord ordained me."

"Anyone could come in here and say that Mr. Rosen."

"But no one did. I have to witness to God."

"We don't have AIDS in our church, Mr. Rosen. We want to keep it that way."

He didn't shake my hand.

So I went to Pastor Buttersmith, who had stayed with me during Shelley's time. He said he would think about it. He said it was a challenge to him. I really wanted to speak in this church. It was the third largest Baptist church in the area, and I had this feeling that God wouldn't let me die until I spoke there. But he said he had to think about it. He thought about it for three months before I understood that there was no way he was going to let me in his church.

 "Ralph, the teacher is coming over to do her laundry."

"The one you met in church?"

"Yes."

"She still doesn't have any children."

"No."

"Is she after the house?"

"No. She's an English teacher. She's different. She's from California."

"Show her the juicer."

"What about the bike?"

"Take her for a ride down the Parkway." He tossed me the keys.

When she came to the house, she looked at the Harley and said she didn't want to take a ride. "I don't take risks," she told me, but she drove me to the junkyard twenty miles out of town where I had seen a 1954 Bentley in a stand of tall grass.

When we got back to the house, I showed her the dryer.

She did her laundry.

Frances from Los Angeles.

A sign or what?

 At the Healing Light Center, that Jewish woman, Judith, told our healing group that she dreaded coming when she thought I would be there. She said this in public. She worshiped New Age beliefs. New Agers believe in karma, that if you had a disease, you must want to be sick or you must have something in your past that you are paying for. Not only did she hate me for being a converted Jew but she also blamed me for my disease.

She said, "Why are you hanging on to your affliction?"

Pedro said to me, "You sound like you love your disease."

"Everyone has problems," Judith said.

"AIDS is a different kind of problem."

"He is totally focused on the disease," Judith said to Father Dan.

"Why don't you concentrate on your attitude," Pedro said, "Have a positive attitude."

"He told other people I am Jewish," said Judith. "That's none of his business, to tell other people."

"It's *her* business to tell other people if she is Jewish or not," Pedro said. "You shouldn't go around telling other people her religion."

"I think you must *want* to be infected," Judith said.

The whole thing made me so sick, I had diarrhea in the church's bathroom for half an hour. The bathroom was set in the room where they served coffee, and the coffeemaker was right by the door. I could hear people coming at the break to get their drinks, talking about what happened, about what Judith said. Some people knocked on the bathroom to see if anyone was in there. There was only one bathroom in the whole place and I couldn't leave.

I never went back there after that.

Frances waited outside on the steps until I came out. She held my hand though we did not pray. She said, "I have some parts to an aquarium."

Ralph and I watch the fish even though the television is on. From across the room on the sofa, I can see the general picture. Ralph sits closer, so he tells me the details, like which fish is eating which other fish. I bought twelve more zebras, which I added to the tank to make a total of eighteen. But the big ones keep picking at a little one, and, by morning, I can count on there being seventeen fish.

"They're going to pick off the little ones," Ralph says about the new fish.

"If they do, I'll dump twice as many fish in there. That'll show them."

"They'll pick off the little ones again, Zack. Use your head."

"I'm trying."

"Try, try, try. You lughead. What'd you do today?"

"Nothing. Sometimes I have dreams of chasing women. But nothing comes out of it. It worries me."

"You mean — come?" Ralph asks.

"That's right, Ralph. I don't even have wet dreams. And I think one of the fish is pregnant. The big one. With the red spot."

"Maybe you should tell Dr. Phillips."

"He's not a vet."

 Gene in my support group said that Alvin used to have it — the CMV that makes you go blind. Alvin got shots directly in his eyes three times a week. He took it with headphones: he put a rock 'n' roll tape into his headset and turned the volume on highest. That was how he stood it, the needles in his eyes. Now, it's different. Now they cut a hole in the jugular vein, fix a valve in the hole, and pump the drug directly into the bloodstream.

That's what they did to me. At first, I carried a pump on my belt to shoot jets of that antiviral into my blood every twelve hours. It was hard to take a shower or go to the bathroom with the portable pump hanging from me on a strap. Now a nurse comes five days a week and plugs me into a pump, infusion it's called, and I get it for one and a half hours a day. No more portable pump. A fork for holding the infusion bag stands next to my fish tank. Usually, during the day, the fork rests in the corner. When the nurse comes she rolls it out, attaches the infusion bag (a special van delivers the drugs once a week for storage in my fridge), and plugs me into it. It feels cold going in.

At first, Dr. Phillips said, "Zack, you'll be on this pump the rest of your life."

But now, I'm not. The system changes. First the pump was attached to my body, and then the pump was stored by my fish tank. My eye doctor, when he first diagnosed the CMV, said, "Zack, you got some cracks in your eyes." Now the cracks are stable but there are cottony patches. He says, "You are holding your own."

I asked Dr. Phillips how long it would take me to go blind if I didn't have the drug. I was thinking that if I was close to the end, I'd want to see all the way to the end. Dr. Phillips didn't want to risk me living the next two years blind because I thought I was going to die and I didn't. I tolerated the pump. It meant hope, a sign that I wasn't going to die tomorrow. As long as Dr. Phillips is worried about my going blind, I know I am going to live.

From the insurance point of view, it was different. The most I could get from them would be half of my death benefits. That's still enough to buy the Harley.

When Frances takes me to the mall to get more fish, I study people and storefronts. I shut my eyes and listen. I've had enough surprises in my life. I don't want to face a new one. I am trying to get ready. I look at all the colors. I listen to the sounds. I am memorizing the world as I know it.

Even going blind, I would die a rich man.

 Frances took me to the mall to get more fish because all the fish died in the tank the day the oil ran out in the house. It was in the middle of winter. With the windchill, it was fifteen below. The TV news showed stories about power lines popping. A quarter of the city remained without power on a Saturday night. My oil ran out.

No one would come out to the house the next day because it was Sunday, and everybody would be in church. Ralph ran water in the sinks all night so the pipes wouldn't freeze. He flushed all the toilets, then shut off the water so it wouldn't break the tank. "If the water freezes in the upstairs john," he said, "you'll know it's really cold." We could see our breath inside the house. We washed all the clothes we could think of just to run the dryer. For a while, we left the stove on with the door open. Then Ralph and I huddled together in the living room, watching television.

"Too bad you can't move into the new house," I said to Ralph.

"Patrice has got to choose."

Even though Patrice has left her husband and moved into the new house alone, she's having second thoughts about Ralph. Her second thoughts have lasted half the winter. Marianne still calls a thousand times a day even though their divorce finally came through.

"What do you think it's going to be, Ralph?"

Before he answered, we suddenly heard a noise, the crash and screeching of metal on metal with sixty-miles-an-hour pushing behind the wheel. Ralph jumped up like it was Marianne calling him.

"Oh, shit," Ralph says, and he goes out the door. "Somebody piled up good."

I was too weak, lying on the sofa. A bowl of soup rested on the floor next to me. My balance has been getting worse. I was afraid of knocking over the soup if I got up. And a bottle of ginger ale. Twelve bottles of pills were on my coffee table. I spent an hour putting them in order, organizing them. Some were tall bottles with child-proof caps. I had Bactrim, prophylactic for pneumonia; something for my dizziness in the head; something for dizziness in the ears; Valium for my nerves, sleeping pills, a pill for my ulcer, vitamins.

What if I went to the window, fell, and knocked all those bottles over? How long would it have taken me to put them all in order again? It would have taken hours, and I was too cold to get out of the covers. Besides, we would have had to turn on all the lights in the house just to see the pills. My eyes were hurting from headaches.

Ralph brought in a wave of cold air when the door slammed behind him. He threw himself into a chair. "Zack, two guys just lost it on the road."

"What? Killed, Ralph?"

"Head on."

"I should call an ambulance. I could make a difference."

"Man, oh man," Ralph said, shaking his head back and forth. "Willie, out back, already called. The conditions those bodies are in, Zack, five minutes won't matter. Nobody could do nothing for those boys."

He saw them. He saw the bodies.

"Just like the deer, Ralph."

"You couldn't have made a difference. No way."

That traffic gets everything that doesn't stay on the road straight enough or fast enough. Deer. Dogs. I once saw my neighbor's cat hit by a spinning wheel. It spun that cat into a rolling ball down the road into the ditch. Cats having nine lives, this cat came out of the ditch on its own, went trotting down the road to my neighbor's house. But you take two young boys behind the wheel, both of them drinking, sleet on the road, and you got a mixture there that doesn't have nine lives. Or five. Or even one between them.

The road department cleaned up the road all night long. We heard them out there, hauling machinery, scraping the road. I never went to the window. All night their lights were reflected through the window in the television. I stayed up late that night, watching television, listening to the sound, trying to keep warm.

Two cars in a head-on collision. The drivers were in their twenties. One driver was drunk. It was the other boys, the passengers, who were killed. Someone erected crosses on the street shoulder across the way.

The crosses on the shoulder bothered Ralph. They were two wooden crosses with names written on them in magic marker. A circle of plastic roses was looped over the top. Every time he came home, he complained about the markers.

"The street looks like a graveyard. Why did they put crosses there?"

Two boys in their twenties. They thought they had their whole lives ahead of them.

"When the snow plow comes, it'll take the markers," Ralph said. He was looking forward to deep snow just for that reason.

"It shows you, Ralph. You never know. I'm the one supposed to die. Nobody goes home early."

■ ■ ■

We were so shook up about the cold and the boys that we forgot about the fish. Because my eyes hurt, the light was off in the tank. We could have put the fish in a bowl and set them on the top of the dryer or the stove. They were so small, we could have thought of something to keep them warm enough to live. We were barely warm enough ourselves. The boys were dead on the road, but we could have saved the fish. It would not have taken so much. Maybe the thought would have been enough, would have been a start.

Dream Number One

I don't know what came over me. Suddenly I got this feeling. I woke up suddenly from a terrible nightmare. It was the worst nightmare I have ever had.

In my dream, my wife died of AIDS, and I had AIDS.

I open my eyes and look around. I feel the bed beneath me. It's a waterbed with the heat turned on too high, so the flannel sheet is soaked. When I awaken, I am soaking wet. I feel the pillow and discover a leak in the waterbed. I see this is my house, although now there is a bannister where there was only an electric extension cord before. Now there is a Jacuzzi where there was only a toilet before.

For a minute, I think it was all a bad dream, and when I get up, I will find Shelley downstairs making coffee. All I have to do is get out of bed and go into the kitchen. But my legs catch at the knees when I try to stand up.

A little voice speaks: *you got AIDS.*

I go through the house throwing things. This is not a dream. I shout everywhere in the house. "Fuck this disease. Fuck you, AIDS."

But my house is in the country. You can play the stereo full blast on fourteen speakers, and no one will hear. Not even the mailman at the mailbox can hear the stereo. I moved here because I wanted to be in the country, away from civilization. I moved here because I wanted to play rock 'n' roll in the country.

Now I find that no one will hear me screaming. Pounding on the bannister. Beating on the wall. Why can't I wake up?

Dream Number Two

I have been having this dream again. In my dream, a wild dog was loose, roaming the countryside. My family got the gun. They were going to shoot the wild dog. This was horrible. First they cut his legs off. It still wasn't enough. It kept running and running, only I'm the one who feels tired, and they cut off its legs. And then they got the gun.

Why do they want to shoot the wild dog?

Dream Number Three

I am in a gurney being wheeled down a corridor at full speed. They have just discovered the cure. In one minute I will die. I jump out of the gurney and run and run. I have to hurry. I have to make it in time. If I don't make it in time . . .

Dream Number Four

Frances and I sit on the front porch of my house and drink tea. Parked in front of the house is a camper. It's got a satellite dish on the top so she can watch her soap operas. A microwave oven. Her portable computer is set up on the dining table inside the camper.

We are resting before we begin our drive to New Mexico. We will go soon. I'll drive, and she can sit at the table and write stories or poems. I keep asking her to write my story, and she says she will one day but can't right now because if she does it will break the mood. Spread out on the backseat are plans for a house. It's a prefab house that I will order. After we find a place in New Mexico, I will sell this old house, buy some property, then build this new house. It will have an independent power source — solar panels and windmills. Ralph will help me build, I know he will. Maybe Patrice will come out to New Mexico for a year and help build this house.

This house will have solar panels and double-glazed windows. It will be a log cabin because wood logs are the best insulation. I'd like a Jacuzzi because I got used to having one. Frances wants all the walls inside painted white. I say OK even though I painted every room in my house with a different color of paint. I know I will be pussy-whipped again, but she's so nice, it's all right.

"The only windmills I know about come from books," she tells me.

"Don't worry," I tell her, "I'll build them."

Dream Number Five

Dream Number five isn't a dream. Technically. I am the dream.

Here is my dream. In which I am the dream.

Frances and Ralph bend over me as I lie on the sofa with the covers pulled up. Because I had chills earlier, Ralph pulled the covers up to my chin. He tucks me in again even though I am already tucked in. Although I am unconscious, I can hear my own snoring.

"Do you think . . . ?" Frances asks. She touches me.

"He gets like that. Feel his shoulder," Ralph tells her.

Both hands are on me but the touch comes from far away. What is happening is that they are touching me, but they aren't exactly touching me.

"He's so cold," she says.

"Feels like a rock," he says.

"Doesn't even look like . . ." she says

"He's alive," he says.

They both sit down on the sofa. They watch me but don't watch me, because I am now like the fish tank, which is all right with me because that means I can be there but I don't have to participate. I don't have to talk, or answer any questions, or make anyone tea. This is a comfortable place to be.

"Zack said you were healed of cancer," Frances says to Ralph.

"I was. I don't know. The Lord had a hand in it."

"What happened? I've never heard the whole story."

"You really want to hear?"

"I do."

Ralph tells his story about the psalm and the surgery. He says, "The day I came home from the hospital and knew I had been saved, I opened my tract, the pamphlet Zack gets, *The Daily Bread* and read the passage for the day. Psalm 103. Do you want to hear it?"

Ralph went to get his Bible, which he keeps in his room. I like it when he reads that psalm. It puts the Lord back into the picture.

His Bible had a zippered case, which he unzips. Then he reads it, but it takes a long time for him to get through because Ralph always cries when he reads it. It has been eight years since he received his healing, and he still starts bawling after the third line.

Ralph and Frances start crying together. He leaves the room to get a roll of paper towels because we have no Kleenex, and at regular intervals, someone pulls a leaf off the roll. Frances blows her nose with a honking noise, Ralph cries like a cat sneezing.

"Do you ever wonder," she starts to ask him, then blows her nose before she finishes, "why you're the one who got a miracle?"

Ralph is still a moment because he's so choked up, then he gets out what is on his mind, which is, "You mean, you wonder if Zack will get one?"

"Kind of."

"No one knows. I didn't deserve it. It just happened. But it says in Scripture, 'Who receiveth much, much is expected of him.' So I know that something is expected of me. I don't know what it is. I just know I am here. Maybe that's what all this is for, that I was supposed to be here and you, in some way, are supposed to be here. Zack's right about the smoking, I know it. 'Much is expected.'"

"Why do you think God hasn't given Zack a miracle?"

"Who knows the mind of God? At first, I kept hoping. But more and more, since he's been on the pump, I have been wondering. It's not over yet. Who knows? If he goes, he promised he'll be the first one I see. He'll be waiting for me when my time comes."

■ ■ ■

I always knew that about Ralph, that he felt that God had given him a miracle for a purpose. Maybe I was his purpose, that he had to see me to the end of something. He tells me I am the best friend he ever had, that I taught him something he never knew before: how to love a man. He didn't even love his father. Ralph calls me "lughead," tells me I am stubborn, but he helps me to the bathroom when I can't walk. The day my leg stopped working in the kitchen when I was standing in front of the fridge, butt naked, he came home for lunch, which he never does. It was totally out of the blue. He just had a feeling he should come home. Then he threw my bathrobe over my shoulders and helped me back to the sofa. He carried me to the tub when I needed a bath, and he soaped up my back for me.

This conversation seems like a dream to me because I am not in it.

I am the dream, and they are the reality.

48 Not everyone gets the chance to start over. The Lord must love me, He gives me so many chances. I believe I still have a chance to preach at New Valley. If the Lord wants me to, He will give the pastor a change of heart. When my health is restored, I will have more of a life with Frances. We will buy a new house with its own power source. I'll get that new bike, the 1986 Harley with gray trim. It will have its own room in the new house. I am still waiting for my life insurance check. I can cash in my life insurance, but if I am healed, I won't have to pay anything back. I would have the money, free and clear. Then I could start my life over again for the second time or the third time. Plus I can get credit.

I asked Frances to marry me three times already. She said no, but she has been with me through all the hard parts. She sticks around to help me and cook and write out my bills. She wrote this for me. When she read part of it back to me, I said, "Frances, you were here in some of these parts, but you wrote it like you weren't here." She said, "This is your story, Zack. And Ralph's." Then she said maybe one day she would write her own story about her experiences, and I said all right. Frances takes me to the store and cooks my meals. When my feet are cold, she sits on the side of the bed, puts my legs in her lap, and rubs my toes. She talks to my legs, saying, "Come on, legs. Come on," rubbing hard till I ask her to stop.

"When my health is restored," I tell her, "I am going to chase you down and marry your ass."

"I'm getting your legs ready for that day," she says.

Ralph said, "Zack, you mangle the English language so much, she must love you."

God gives everyone a measure of life. With most people, it takes a whole measure of life to live a whole life. Most people finish school, get married, have children. They do all the things they are supposed to in the time God gives. They know what is important, who to love, who to marry, how to get an education, what stocks to invest in. Like my brothers. Their lives were full to the top, but they didn't understand that.

There are a lot things I never did. I never rode a horse. I never voted or read a poem. I never got a passport. I never went to New Mexico. I never finished my high school education. I had a wasted youth. I had a miserable job for many years. I loved a woman who lied to me. I did crazy things in my youth, having no positive purpose because of drinking and drugging. I tore up some good cars even though I made a fine Harley from parts.

Only near the end did I really start to understand things. I stopped looking for direct directions from God. I used to think that all signs had meanings attached to them, but I now think the meaning is there without the signs. I watch the stars without trying to interpret them. I watch the snow for crocus to shoot out. When the snow has melted, I watch for the robins to come and dig out worms from the muddy ground. I watch for flood to guard my weeping willow. I watch for spring and the weeds growing in the ditch. I watch for the ladybugs swarming round my kitchen fan. Day after day, I count daffodils as they appear, so I know the new ones. I watch the night for my destiny, like a bridegroom (as we are to watch, says the Lord) in readiness for his bride.

Most people take their whole life to live their whole life. But if you could squeeze your life up into a ball, and live the whole measure at the end, you could accomplish something glorious.

For the Lord.

Afterword

In matters of faith, I was very different from Zack, as indeed, I differed from him a thousand ways culturally and educationally, but he was my friend and he was my hero, not so much for the tenets of faith he espoused as for the nobility and courage he brought to bear on his experience. He expected nothing from others but accepted everything with joy. Although Zack sometimes wondered why his fate befell him as it did, he never doubted that God had a purpose for him. Except those times he endured profound physical pain, he cried for others, not for himself. In fact, he imagined other people suffered more than he did.

While Zack was alive, Ralph and I worked out a care-giving partnership though we never planned or discussed it. Ralph took care of Zack when he was home. Ralph cleaned the bathroom when Zack had accidents. He picked Zack up off the floor when he fell in the middle of the night. Ralph bathed him, fed him, took care of the house, and loved him fully as a friend. For Ralph and Zack, faith was less a state of being than it was an activity in life; thus Ralph coined the verb "christianize" to describe their mutual exchange of faith. I took Zack to the doctor, fed him, brought him to my house on weekends, managed his correspondence, and did whatever else I could. I held his medical power of attorney until June 1, 1995. When Zack began to suffer progressively with dementia, Ralph and I tried to make sure that one of us stayed with him or knew where he was when he went to give "speaks" or visit friends.

As of the completion of this manuscript, Ralph lives with Patrice in the house they built together.

At the time of Zack's death, his parents were alive but in ill health and living in different parts of the country. Although his father suffered from chronic mental illness, he remained resolute in his efforts to influence legislation requiring a blood test for AIDS prior to the issuance of a marriage license.

Zack's siblings, a sister and the two brothers, live in different parts of the Eastern Seaboard. Zack's foster family continues to reside in New Jersey.

Zack learned that he had CMV, the virus that leads to blindness in persons with AIDS, on December 26, 1994. In May 1995, he was hospitalized for a potassium deficiency. He never returned home after that.

As long as I knew him, Zack wanted to die at home. He told this to everyone: Ralph, his friends, his doctors, his family. He told me he wanted to be buried in purple. Before he died, he asked Pastor Johnny to preach the eulogy at his funeral; he wanted Ralph and me to attend as well.

On June 1, 1995, Frankie, Zack's younger brother, came from Atlanta to secure Zack's medical and legal powers of attorney. Frankie moved Zack to an Atlanta nursing home on July 10, 1995. Zack died two weeks later on July 24, 1995.

None of his last wishes were honored.